TRENT

CALHOUN MEN BOOK 1

KATHI S. BARTON

This is a work of fiction. Names, characters, places, and incidents are products of the author's imagination or are used fictitiously and are not to be construed as real. Any resemblance to actual events, locations, organizations, or persons, living or dead, is entirely coincidental.

World Castle Publishing, LLC
Pensacola, Florida
Copyright © Kathi S. Barton 2016
Hardback ISBN: 9781629893709
Paperback ISBN: 9781629893716
eBook ISBN: 9781629893273
First Edition World Castle Publishing, LLC, January 11, 2016
http://www.worldcastlepublishing.com
Licensing Notes
Cover: Karen Fuller
Editor: Eric Johnston
Editor: Maxine Bringenberg

PROLOGUE

1224 AD

Johanna, Joe to her few friends, moved as quickly as she could to the heap of trash that had been put out only moments ago. It might have been filled with nothing more than a few scraps of food, but it would be enough to fill the hole that seemed to be forever in her belly. And maybe if she was lucky enough, she'd find a pair of shoes with only a few holes in them, or a coat. But before she could get close enough to see, she saw Abraham and another man. It did not look to her as if they were friends.

At first she thought they were having relations. It wouldn't surprise her if they were. Abraham would do most anything for a bit of coin or food. She did not care for the man overly much, but she would help to keep him safe even if the man didn't seem to think he needed her. But before she could move around the two of them, she saw that Abraham held a man at knife point.

The man he held she did not know, but she did know what he was. A vampire. There were plenty of them about now, feeding on ones such as herself and Abraham when they needed food. While she knew very little about his kind, she did know that he would kill the man that held him if he only moved just a little. Looking into his eyes, she spoke to him.

"Please do not harm him." The man stilled in his slight struggle to look at her. "He is only hungry, as are the rest of us, and would otherwise leave you alone."

"He has a bit of coin, Joe. More than we could have a fine meal on. I'll share it with you should you help me. I promise I will this time." Joe looked at Abe and shook her head. "You just stand there and I'll slice his throat and we'll find us a meal, you and me."

"Abe, this man has done nothing to you save come to this place of death and sadness. Let him go before he hurts you." To the man, she spoke again. "Please. Do not harm him. He is not a nice person, but he is all that I have here."

Blood moved down the handsome man's throat, staining the collar of his white silk shirt. Joe knew that just the cost of his shirt would have fed her and Abe for many days. His small nod was all she needed to let out the breath that she'd been holding. Looking at Abe again, she took a step toward him, speaking softly, her hand guiding his away from the throat of the stranger.

"You don't want to kill him, Abe. Should you do that, the food that you eat from this will taste bitter and will make you sick for a long while. You know this." Abe growled at her, telling her to go away. "I cannot and you know that. Should this man kill you for what you have done, then I will have one less person that I know here, and I have so few now. Please, let him go so that you and I can go to the dump that is still warm from the house."

She didn't think he was going to do it. He looked determined, his face set. When his belly growled, hers did as well. It was a sound that she was sick of. When Abraham stomped his foot at her, she wanted to remind him that he was a grown man and that he should act like one.

"I need a fine meal, Joe. I was never meant to be like this. I am a great man." She'd heard the stories before. He'd come from a grand house, the servant to a great man. But it was, like other stories she'd heard in her life, a lie. A fabrication of something that was a dream to him, a way to make him seem more important than he really was. But his lies, like his stories, had long since given her a headache. Joe had given up on dreams. They were useless without any way of making them a reality. "I will make his death quick if that would make you feel better."

"Nay, it will not and you will know it." Joe glanced at the man, who watched her carefully. "Allow this man to go about his business. Perhaps he will give you a coin or two for your troubles. Would you let him go for that?"

"I should have it all." Joe shook her head and told him to be reasonable. "I am not going to let him go without all his coin, Joe. You cannot ask me to do such a thing. It has been years since —"

"Then I will quit you." He looked at her then. "I will no longer come to your aid should you become ill again. I will not give you a part of my blanket when I have none to share with even myself. You will be on your own. And you know that no one else will help you either, Abe. You have made many enemies here."

Taking the last two steps to the two of them, she put her hand on Abe's hand again. When he didn't fight her, she moved the handmade silver blade from the man's throat, but did not look at him. As soon as he was free he leapt from them, then fell to the ground. Joe stood in front of Abe.

"Please don't harm him. He is starved." The man held his neck and nodded while blood poured from between his fingers. She knew that he would die soon. No matter what he was he should get himself healed or he would bleed out and die there as the sun came up to take him. "I will trade myself for him."

"Send him away." The voice was cultured, hard, and full of hate. Her fear of the man, now that he was free, doubled. "Send him away, Joe, and come to me."

Nodding, she turned to Abe and then back to the man. "Coin. Do you have a coin or two that you can spare to give to him? I should hate to have lied to him."

He reached into his pocket and pulled out a very beautiful change purse. She could tell that it had been made with a fine hand, and that the beading work alone was done by someone who loved their job. If only she could have such a job. Shutting down that thought, she reached for the three coins in his palm and took only the two that she'd promised Abe he could have. The man grabbed her hand before she could move away.

"Give them all to him." She shook her head and turned to Abe. Giving him the two gold coins, she turned back to the man when he said her name. "Why did you not take the three of them, if only to have one for yourself?"

"I did not say that I would take one for myself. I do not lie. No matter how hungry I am." He nodded, his face pale now. "What do I need to do to help you?"

"You would still come to me, even with your friend safe?" She told him that Abe was not her friend. "Then pray, why did you save him?"

"I did not want him dead by your hand. I do not want anyone dead by your hand. Your kind have been killing us off for years, and I should like to be able to think I have saved one. Even if it was just Abe the thief." He nodded but said nothing more. "What do you need of me?"

"You know what I am, so you know what I need." She nodded and moved closer to him. "Come to me. I should like to have you drink from my wound if only to draw some of the poison that Abe has put inside of me. The silver of it even now is racing in my veins to kill me."

He was weaker than she'd thought. But she knew that even in his weakened state, he could still kill her. Once, not long ago, she'd seen one of his kind tear a man's head off even with a stick protruding from his belly. And then he'd stood and pulled it from him as he drank greedily from another that stood too close.

Moving to sit on the ground near him, Joe leaned into his neck and could smell his soap. Not that she'd had any chance to have such a thing. She tried her best to make her way to the river at least once a week, no matter what the weather was, to clean herself and her clothing as best she could.

As soon as she put her mouth over the large cut, he curled his hand in the back of her head and pulled her tightly against him. His blood didn't taste as she'd thought it might. There was a coppery tang to it, but it was warm and filled her belly nicely. Trying not to think of what she was doing, she lifted her head from his neck when he lifted her and fitted her over his lap. Her legs on either side of his hips, she was in a position that she was sure was going to get her raped if not killed.

"I shall not take what is not freely given to me." Nodding, she watched his eyes as they darkened. "If you are coming when I drink from you, I will not need as much to fill me to heal. Do you know what I am asking you to do?"

"You wish to have sex with me?" He nodded, then shook his head. "I do not understand you. Should you not like to have sex with me? I am free of diseases. Not that I wish to have it with you, but I did give myself to you in Abe's place."

"I only wish for you to come for me. Have your pleasure as if we were having sex." Joe still had no idea how that worked. "And I am aware of your body. Not only are you free of anything that would kill you, but you are a virgin as well. I would guess you have had to work very hard to keep yourself in such a state."

"There are not a lot of men that wish to touch someone such as me." He asked her why. "I'm not what is considered a very well-endowed woman. I am…too skinny, and most think me a boy."

"You are not a boy, and that would not stop most men that I know should you have happened to be one." He watched her face and she felt herself heat in embarrassment. "You are very strange, Joe. A human that would help a vampire even though you know that it could cost you your life."

"I have not much of one anyway, my lord. This is all that I have." He pulled her body to his again; this time she could feel his hardness. "You wish me to come, but as you have said, I have no knowledge of how this will work."

"I will do the work, little one. You will be my savior and I will give you pleasure." His laughter made her hurt with anger, but he only pulled her to him again. "I should like nothing more than to show you the delights of having me inside of you, but if I do not feed from you soon, I will still be here when the sun rises. Tilt your head for me and I shall bring you to peak. Your blood will be much stronger and tastier for it."

Tilting her head as he had directed her to, Joe felt the heat of his breath on her. When his tongue lapped at her pounding pulse, she put her hands on his shoulders to hold on for the pain of what he was going to do. As surely as she was sitting atop the man, she knew that he was going to kill her.

The bite was gentle, almost like a deep kiss. And when he drew deeply on her throat, taking her blood into his mouth, she moaned before she could think that he'd hear her. As he pulled her to him again, she could feel his hardness getting thicker, his manhood touching something deep within her even though she was as dressed as he was.

When he commanded her to come, Joe found herself rolling her hips up to his body, riding him, she supposed. The feeling that he was giving her, the way that his hardness kept pressing against her womanhood, made her hold tighter to him. She knew that something was going to happen and it was going to tear her apart. As soon as she felt it take her, the feeling that she'd been reaching for, her scream of release — for that was all she could think of it being — nearly had her sobbing.

~~~

Noah drank deeply of her. She tasted like a fine wine to him, her blood spiked with her release as well as the virginity of her body, something he'd not had in more years than he could remember. As she rode him faster, coming again and again, he knew that he could take her, slam his cock deep within her and she'd let him. But, like her, he'd made a promise, and Noah prided himself on his word. But to have her, all of her, was making him greedy for more. When she went limp in his arms, he knew that he'd taken too much from her weak and starved body. And the numerous releases had taken their toll on her. He had to save her, even if it was from herself.

Sealing the wound at her throat, he looked at her. She was pretty in a too thin sort of way. And the fact that she believed that men thought her a boy had him thinking that she had something inside of her that kept her from harm. But someday, and he'd bet soon, she would run out of whatever it was and she would be as dead as most of the humans in this part of town. Laying her beside him on the ground, Noah stood up and took to the skies to free himself of the stench of the man who had held him.

He should have killed the man, and it had been his intention. But he'd heard her coming toward them and had paused to see if she'd be a tastier meal. When she pleaded so prettily for the man's life, not only had Noah been impressed, but he'd been curious as well. Especially when she'd told him that the man was not her friend. Going back to the place he'd left her, Noah did the only thing he could do...he picked her up in his arms and took her to his home.

"My lord." His butler and friend Michael looked at the woman, then backed away from her. She did smell, but not as badly as he'd smelled many times before. "You have killed her? And why, pray tell, have you brought her body here?"

"Nay. I have brought her here because...well, I'm not sure why I have. But I should like to have her fed and well bathed. She saved my life tonight." Michael looked at him, then at the girl with a new kind of interest. "Had she not taken my blood into hers to drain the poison of silver from my body, then fed me, you would have been without a master and I would be like the dust that is now on my boots."

He carried her up to the second floor. Michael was asking him what had happened, and he told him everything. The man had been in his service for many years and there was nothing that the man did not know about him. He was, in a word, his friend. His only one, he supposed.

Noah didn't know why he'd never been into nests of his kind. But as soon as he was able, he'd left his home, the one his father was the lord of, and set out to find his own way. Never once had it occurred to him to gather his own bunch of vampires to live and be with him, preferring to be in his own home with servants that he trusted. That had been nearly five centuries ago, and in all that time he'd lived alone but for the five people in his household. Each of them humans at one time, and as loyal to him as he was them.

"I shall have someone come and bring her something clean to wear. Perhaps we can borrow a few things from the cook in the meantime." Noah nodded as he lay her on the large bed, looking bigger for the fact that she was so tiny.

"She is very tall, is she not?" Yes, Noah thought, she was very tall, but still very small in that she was thin. Much too thin. "I will have the cook make her something to eat. It will be strange, my lord, having her here."

"It will be." Pulling the blanket up and over her body, it occurred to Noah that he'd never said she was going to live there, but now that it was said, he realized that had been his intention all along. To help her as she had him. "Michael, what do you suppose we should do with her? She is...she is very protective of anyone, even me."

"I should think she'd make a wonderful day walker for you, my lord. You know that the household would do anything for you, but it would lessen our burden a little should we have her to do that job for us." Noah only looked at his friend with a cocked brow. "I am not saying that we do not love doing it, but she needs to have a job and this would be a good one for her. I have not met her, but I would be willing to bet that she will need a purpose or she will not stay."

It was funny that Michael would know that about her. She would, too, need a job to keep her busy, or she'd think she was taking advantage of him. Or him her. And he might need her again, just to replenish himself. But he'd never spoil her. That was not his to take, and he would never do that to her. Tempting as she was, he was a man of honor.

CHAPTER 1

Present Day

Trent entered his office and turned to leave again. Seeing his dad there was enough to send him running in the other direction. Today especially. It was hot and humid, and all Trent wanted to do was go home, curl up on his new couch, and enjoy his air-conditioning. His new everything, including his house, was calling to him.

"Oh, don't be like that. I brought you a peace offering. And how many times must I tell you that I'm sorry before you forgive me?" Trent pretended to think on that. "Damn it, boy, I didn't know she was gonna do that. I only wanted you to have a nice date."

"You set me up with a hooker, Dad. How the hell did you expect the night to end? With me getting married to her?" His dad mumbled something about how his mom was still mad too, but Trent ignored it. "You should be ashamed of yourself. What the hell were you thinking?"

"I wasn't thinking she was a hooker, that's for sure. I just wanted to make you less tense." If his dad thought that was helping; he was sadly mistaken. "I got you something. I know you're gonna forgive me when you see it."

Trent was still standing in the doorway and lifted his nose to the air to see if he could— "Biscuits? You got me...where did you get them?"

He was moving into the room when his dad pulled the towel off the still steaming treat. It was his biggest downfall, biscuits. He could eat them with every meal...hell, even eat them for his entire meal, but he also knew that they were bad for him. Especially the way that he ate them.

Drowning in butter and marmalade, with just a hint of honey over them, was the only way, as far as he was concerned, that biscuits should ever pass over one's lips. He sat down at his desk when he saw the dozen round treats with a jar of marmalade and a squeeze bottle of pure honey. He looked at his dad when he laughed. He wasn't ready to forgive him just yet, but it was getting close. Trent asked him again where he'd gotten them.

"We have a visitor while Meggie is laid up with her sore back. Her niece or something is filling in for her. I came into the kitchen yesterday to these babies, and I thought of you. Had her make me up a batch just for you." Trent no more believed that than he did his dad was sorry about two nights ago. "I really did think of you."

"How many did you have her bake up so that these were left over, Dad? And why is Mom letting you eat like this?" His dad snorted but didn't answer. Trent picked up the first biscuit and held it to his nose. "Holy shit, Dad. These even smell sinful."

"They are. And your mother, she can eat a dozen of them, so you know. And this girl's scones. Never had them before, but I'm betting that there isn't a shop around that can do them up better. Go ahead and eat it. See if I'm not right." Trent took a healthy bite of the one in his hand. His taste buds exploded in his mouth, and he moaned. "Didn't I tell you? I swear to you, those could be considered lethal if you ate enough of them. Damned if I can't eat me one more."

Trent pulled the plate back when his dad reached for them. "Mine. Get your own. These are my peace offering, remember?"

His dad sat down while Trent ate two more before he opened the jar of marmalade and honey. He almost hated to taint the taste of the perfection that the biscuits were, but knew that he had to try one with his favorite things on them. He heard his brother Elijah talking to his secretary in the hall and actually considered hiding his treat. But he knew that if he did, in about ten minutes he'd be full and sick to his belly, and the thought of not having these again made him leave them on his desk. But he did slip two into his top drawer with the towel.

"There are ninety-seven thousand ways I can kill that man right now, and one of them is simply shifting to my wolf and tearing his throat out. What a...what are you eating?" Elijah looked at the plate in front of him with only two biscuits left on it then at his dad. "You bribed him? You actually went out and paid someone to bake him biscuits to get him to talk to you again. And you think this will work? He's really pissed off at you."

"Eat this and shut up." Trent shoved the plate at his brother and nearly snatched it back when he took both of the biscuits left on the plate. He was never going to do that again, that was for sure.

When he sat down and ate the first one in a single bite, Elijah looked at his dad. "Okay, this will work. Holy hell, Dad, where did you get these?" Elijah enjoyed a good biscuit too, but not like Trent did. He'd write a bad review for a breakfast place if their biscuits were not up to his standards. And he had high ones too. As he ate the second one, Trent pulled one of his stash from his drawer and ate it while their dad explained.

"Meggie hurt her back a few days ago, and her relative was in town or something so she said she could help her out. And damn, this girl can cook. Your mom said that if she could do it without hurting Meggie's feelings, we'd just keep this girl. Of course, we'd be as big as a house then, but it'd be well worth it." Trent thought so, too, but was too busy trying to stuff the last of his stash in his mouth before Elijah took it. "I can bring you in some more tomorrow if you like. The girl loves to help this old man out."

"You told her what you did?" His dad blushed bright red. "You mean you didn't tell your now favorite cook that you hired a hooker to entertain me for the night and then were surprised when you had to explain to Mom why I was so pissed off? And nearly had to bail me out of jail when she started screaming that I'd tried to stiff her? Christ, Dad, she was naked in my bed before I even got my jacket on to go out to dinner with her. Not to mention, I think she stole my cuff links. And I'm not even going to try and guess where she might have hidden them to get them out of my apartment. All I can say to you is you're lucky that I don't live there anymore. I'm pretty sure that she's cased the place, and I would have been robbed blind by now."

"I'm telling you, I didn't know nothing about her other job." Trent snorted. "Well, I didn't. I knew that she was working for some guy and that she went on dates and stuff, but I didn't know that's what she did. You have to believe me, and tell your mom that you do."

"Mom is mad at you?" His dad nodded and looked pretty sad about it. "Good. My God, Dad, do you have any idea what she wanted me to...? What she suggest...? Never mind. I think you should be in trouble with Mom a little bit longer. This might teach you to stop meddling in the lives of your sons."

"I doubt that." Trent had to agree with his brother. Their dad was forever trying to set them up with women. As if any of them had any trouble in that department. Trent didn't date much, but when he wanted to go out, there were countless women that would go with him. And if he wanted to get laid, as his father had arranged unknowingly for him, he didn't have to worry about what sort of things she was bringing with her. Such as handcuffs and cock locks, whatever the fuck those were.

"You do know that I'm not getting any younger." Elijah told him if he tried that trick on him, he'd not get any older either. "I won't. You got my promise on that one. I'll be careful. I learned my lesson. I don't get my sons dates with women of the street. Yeah, but you have to admit, she sure was a pretty little thing."

"There was very little about her that was little."

Trent looked at the door when someone cleared their throat and saw his mom there. Feeling his face heat up, he told her he was sorry and invited her into to have a seat.

"I'm guessing that you've forgiven your father now?" Trent told him he wasn't sure. "I should hope that you'd make him dangle on that particular hook for a while yet. The nerve of him thinking you needed that sort of help when it came to women. I've not been speaking to him since I heard about this. TJ, I swear to you that if you do this again, I will not just leave you, I will make you regret it for a very long time."

"I already said that I wouldn't. And I did try to make it up to him." They all turned to see the now empty plate on his desk. "He surely did like those biscuits, just like I said he would. And if he dated more, I'd not have to go to extreme measures to get him a mate."

"I don't need help at all with women. I know how to treat them." His mom glared at him, but all Trent did was wink at her. "Tell me about this woman who can bake for you like she did my biscuits. Is she looking for work?"

"No. I don't think so. Meggie told me that she was here helping her out and that she'd taken time from her job to do so. You should talk to her, Trent. Very nice and polite. And I'm fairly certain she doesn't make her living taking on the male clientele she finds on the street." Trent burst out laughing, but stopped quickly when his mother looked at him. "Be that as it may, she is a very nice girl. Pretty too. But I do think she's been in the area more than we thought. She knows the town as well as we do. I've no details, but Meggie said that she was her only true friend and that she loved her like her own daughter. I do think that Meggie has three of her own, so that's not saying much. Meggie doesn't care at all for her children on most days."

"They're close then." His mom said that they seemed to be. That when Meggie had called, she'd dropped everything to come help her. "What's her name? I can see what our realtor has on the list if she doesn't have a home here. We mostly only deal with business zoned property, but we might be able to find something for her. What's her name?"

"Joe Samuels. I'm not sure of too much more about her. There is a vampire in her life, but I have no idea if he's just another friend or not. She's certainly not sleeping with him." To Trent that meant the girl was a virgin. He wondered how much she resembled her male name, or if she was still a virgin because she took after her aunt.

Meggie was a wonderful person, but she looked like she could beat a bear with a switch and come out on top.

"I know. Come out for dinner tomorrow night." His mom nodded at Dad's suggestion. "All of you. I'll make some calls and we'll have a big family gathering. It'll be good for us too, what with Tanner home for good now and Sterling finally getting out of his funk."

"Trent James Calhoun, what a thing to say." His dad looked like he was going to ask what he'd said, but one look at Mom had him dropping his head. "In the event you don't remember, Sterling has been down in the *dumps* for a while because he was in an accident. And it's not dumps, you idiot, but pain. I cannot believe you at times."

As they left them, his mom still fussing at his dad as they walked out of the door, Trent decided to get to work. Elijah sat in the chair across from him and seemed content not to speak. As the computer finished up the reboot that had started as he was leaving last night, he thought of his family.

There were six of them, the sons of his parents. Trent was the oldest, of course. Then there was Sterling, Scott, Randal, Elijah, and Tanner bringing up the rear. He loved them all dearly and would do anything for them, as he was sure they would for him. As a wolf family, purebloods that had been wolves for generations, they were all very close. Trent looked at his brother when he cleared his throat.

"I need to tell you something about Max Ford. The guy we're trying to deal with on the loan." Trent noticed that he had seven emails from the man and told Elijah that. "Yeah, he's a little upset with us. You mostly. I hope you don't mind, but I had to use you as a heavy yesterday. We can't do business with a man like him. Not only that, but—"

"You know that's all right. What happened?"

21

Elijah got up to pace. Not a good sign. His brother and he had been in business for the last ten years...since the year that Elijah had turned twenty-one and come into his inheritance from their grandmother.

"He's been robbing from the company. We knew that he was having problems, and he told us it was the economy, but what we didn't know was that he's stealing the money and sending it overseas so that no one can get to it. I think he's playing us to fund his trip over there to live in the lap of luxury and stiff us with the bill. Also, I've only just found out he's not been paying into the retirement funds of any of the people that work for him. His partner has no idea, I don't think, but that's not all of it. He's stealing from his own accounts as well, from what I can see, and funneling that to his accounts. I mean, it's bad enough that he's skipped out on taxes on both his person and businesses, but to hurt the very people that have worked for you for years is pretty shitty." Trent asked him where his heavy hand came in. "I told him that we decided not to lend him any money at this time. I never gave him a reason. You and I discussed that before, and I remembered you telling me that we didn't have to have a reason, that we're just not going to do it. I'm thinking it'll be like forever before we lend him money, but we'll cross that bridge later. Oh, and I think he might come in today. I had everyone tell him we had no appointments, but I don't think that's going to stop him from coming and begging."

Trent didn't say anything. He'd missed that when he'd been going over the paperwork for Ford's firm. And that was a huge deal. They would have lost a great deal of money on that deal had they gone through with it. Not that they couldn't take the hit. They had insurance for that, but he'd missed it. Trent thought he'd been doing that a lot lately.

And while he was thinking about what his brother said to him, two more emails came in from the very man they were talking about. They could just walk away from this deal, of course, but the problem was how much they had invested in this venture to get to the point where they were right now. Just about to the point where they were signing off on it. Hundreds of thousands of dollars.

"All right. Then it's done."

Trent felt his belly tense up and his heart pound in his chest as soon as the words left his mouth. He knew that Elijah could hear it and hoped that he thought it was just a simple case of nerves. But Trent knew better. As he tried to slow his heart and breathing, he began to see pinpoints of light in his vision.

This had happened to him several times over the last few weeks. He'd be out of breath for a few minutes just walking from the couch to the kitchen. His head would spin and he'd feel sick. But the way his heart was pounding right now he was a little afraid, and he knew it was making his heart beat all the faster. Soon he couldn't see anything but what looked like blood rushing behind his eyelids.

He heard his name being called, screamed really, and Trent felt his body sliding to the floor as his heart started to ache. His chest felt as if it were going to explode, and he knew that he was dying. Right there, right then, he was dying. Closing his eyes against the unrelenting pain, Trent tried to think, about anything other than how badly his chest was hurting, how his arms were going numb, and how his head felt as if someone had shot a cannon off in it. But all he could think about was that he hurt and he was too young to die. Looking at the face that seemed to fade in and out in front of him, he told his mom that he loved her and simply passed out.

~~~

Joe counted as she did the compressions on the big man's chest. Each time she thought she couldn't go any further, she'd glance at the face of the man's mother and double her efforts to bring him around. He would not die while she was there to help, not if she could help it.

She'd only come by to get a ride back to the estate with the Calhoun's. They'd said they were coming into town to see their sons, and she knew that one of them worked in the big building. Having gained access to the upper floors, she was nearly bowled over by Mr. Calhoun when he was rushing by her to this office. When she entered too, it took her breath away to see the younger man on the floor and no one doing a damned thing to help him.

"The ambulance just pulled up." Joe nodded at Elijah, the man she'd been introduced to when she'd told him to get the fuck out of her way. No one, it seemed, had ever taken a first responder class and they were too stunned to even call out for help. "I'm really sorry."

Nodding, she kept at her work. The small mask that had been placed over the man's mouth had come from the kit that was brought to her when she had to give him mouth to mouth. The secretary had said that she could help, but she wasn't sure if she could do that to her boss. Joe thought she'd fire the dumbass if it were her decision. What kind of person didn't want to help their boss?

By the time the medical team showed up, Mr. and Mrs. Calhoun had stopped sobbing about their little boy, and Elijah had called the others. Joe wasn't sure who that might be, but she was pretty sure that they might be family. Mr. Calhoun had told her that he had a big family, and Mrs.

Calhoun had told her that they had six sons. If this was one of them, he had to take better care of himself if he wanted to be around for a while.

Joe moved back out of the way to let the men who were paid to do this step in. She watched the man that she'd worked so hard to save. He was still breathing, which was good, and his color had improved a great deal since she'd come in. All good signs for someone who more than likely had suffered a heart attack.

He was handsome...a big guy with a short military type hair cut that made him look younger than the thirty-three she'd been told he was. He wasn't heavy by any means. In fact, his body was toned and well-muscled. When she'd pulled his shirt open to keep his heart pumping, Joe had been surprised to find his chest smooth, free of the fur that she had always associated with wolves. Knowing what he was, Joe had figured he'd be hairy.

"Joe?" She looked over at Mr. Calhoun and nodded. "They want us to go with them. Can you come along? I'd really like for you to be with us being that he's only here on account of your quick thinking."

She doubted that. Joe was sure that someone would have stepped up had she not knocked them out of the way when he'd first fallen. Shaking her head, she started to tell them that she needed to get home to her aunt, but Mrs. Calhoun insisted.

"My aunt will worry." Mrs. Calhoun told her she'd call. "I really don't want to intrude, Mrs. Calhoun. I know that you need to be together as a family."

"Had you not been here, we'd not be much of a family." Joe tried to tell her that she'd only been the first to try. "No. That's not true. We were standing there like fish out of water, not sure how to save him. I would really like for you to go too. Just in the event that the doctor has any questions for us."

In the end, she went with them. It seemed that for every excuse that she had, they countered her with a good reason. Besides, they were her only ride home. Going with them seemed easier than trying to walk home. Not that she couldn't do it. She was in good shape, but it was about eight miles in the heat.

They were all there by the time she and his parents arrived. Four men the size of the Calhoun's filled the waiting room, and adding the other one and the dad and mom, the room felt positively packed. Standing in the hall, trying to not be overwhelmed by them all, brought her face to face with a man she'd just as soon not ever see again.

"Well, well, well." Joe started to back away from Max Ford, but found herself hitting a wall of a chest behind her. When hands held her arms, it was everything she could do not to try and run. "Look what the cat dragged in. It's the little bitch that thinks she can tell me what to do. What do you think, David? Should we teach her a lesson right now? She sure did think herself pretty grand the other week when I only wanted to talk to her roommate. What's old Noah doing with himself nowadays? Still letting you run things for him?"

"Let her go, Ford." No one moved at the sound of the voice next to her. Joe didn't turn to look. She knew Mr. Calhoun's voice when she heard it. One thing about the man, he could talk your arm off when he thought he had something to say. Or even not. The man could jabber on and on. "You heard me. I said to let her go. She's here with my family."

"Your family?" Joe said nothing, but she knew that the rest of them, all the Calhoun's, had joined their patriarch. "I had no idea that she walked in those circles, TJ. I was just going to tell her that we're ready for her to come and work for us now that we've gotten some things straightened out. With your son there helping us with the loan he said we could have, we'll be able to afford her."

"You've yet to unhand her. And we've been about as polite as I think we need to be on this." This was from the man that she'd knocked down, Elijah. "Let her go, or the only thing saving your life will be the fact that we're this close to the emergency room."

She was let go, but shoved just hard enough to nearly fall when she staggered. Elijah put his hands out to stop her descent to the floor. As he held her to him, three of the others, their names escaping her memory right now, stood between her and Max, and his sometimes bodyguard, David.

"For some reason, and this could just be me, I'm thinking that she doesn't want to work for you. Is that right, Joe?" She nodded at Elijah. "See? She doesn't want to work with you either. And I'm pretty sure my brother and I have made it perfectly clear that we have no desire to help you out. Not now and not ever. Now, I think you should move on your way and leave us on our own."

"Can't blame a man for trying, now can you? I've heard nothing but good things about how Miss Samuels can turn a dime into a buck. Besides, I thought you were gonna talk to that brother of yours about our business. I went by the offices and saw them wheeling him out, and came here to see if I could offer up some assistance. I had no idea that you knew Joe here. I've been after her to work for me for years now." No one said a word, and Joe moved back a little more, freeing herself from Elijah, only to be pulled closer to Mrs. Calhoun. "I'm still a little in the dark as to

27

why we've all decided this won't work. All we had left to do was sign off on some papers and it was a merger made in heaven."

"I've already told you that we've decided against it. That should be enough for you to move on. It was for us." Max looked at her, and she could see the hatred in his eyes. There had been no time when she'd been going to work for him. And Joe had no idea why he'd said that to them. "Unless you have business elsewhere on this floor, Ford, I'd really like it if you left us on our own. We're here for our brother and not to explain to you about why no means no."

As soon as Elijah turned his back on the man, it was as if the rest of them had some sort of inner connection, and they all turned as well. Max tried to talk to her again when they moved back into the small room.

"You talk to that boss of yours before—"

That was as far as he got before she was pulled into the room with the rest of the Calhoun's. Simon stood near enough that should Max have tried anything, he would have been thwarted in his efforts.

Max watched her as he made his way to the elevator, glancing back over his shoulder every few minutes. She wasn't afraid of him, but she was afraid of what he might try to do to the Calhoun's and to Noah.

Max had changed a great deal, but she knew who he was. Not only that, Noah did as well. A man could change himself whenever and however he wanted, but his scent would forever be the same. She knew who he was because Noah had smelled him on her when Max had accosted her the other day when she'd been in town for groceries. She thought about Noah now, and decided he needed to have a heads up on the fact that Max was trying his crap again.

Not to mention, he was trying to insert himself into the Calhouns' lives as well.

The man Ford is threatening me and you. Again. Noah asked her where she was. *Mercy General Hospital. One of the people that I have been helping had a heart problem, and I was there with them. The Calhouns. You heard Meggie talking about them. Max knows them as well, but they do not know him as we do. He is expecting them to finance something for him. That can only mean trouble for the pack. They are a good family, and I hate to think of what Ford can do to them.*

Meggie wasn't her aunt, not really. Joe had no living relatives. And had she any when she'd been younger, they had all long since died. Meggie was the descendant of the sister of Michael, the man that had worked for Noah as his keeper longer than Joe had. They all had been watching over the family for generations, and when Meggie had started working for the Calhouns, they knew the family inside and out before she ever made their first meal for them. She had always been a firm believer, as had Noah, that they cared for their own.

I will be there soon. The wolves, are they as good as we have thought? A pack that might be open to me coming to see them? She told them that they were. *You will please warn them that I will come by soon. I know that I need no permission to visit there, but I should ask that you tell them. I don't wish for any hard feelings even before we begin.*

I will. They saved me, I think. Noah asked her how, and she told him what happened. *They had no reason to do that, Noah. They owe me nothing.*

You think no one owes you anything when I know for a fact that I owe you my life several times over. She told him she loved him, and to her that was reason enough to risk her life for him over and over. *Yes, child, and I you, but there is the added fact that you have saved me a great many times.*

After telling him where they were in the big hospital, he told her that he'd come soon. She turned to the family and tried to think how to tell them he was coming. The best way, she'd always found, was usually the simplest. Just straight out.

"Have you heard of Noah Stark?" Most of them had and Joe nodded. "He is the man that I watch over when he needs me to. I have been his for a great many years. We have been...friends. He should like to come here and talk with you. All of you." She explained that they both knew Max Ford, and they might want to listen to him. "Noah is a good man."

"He's a vampire, isn't he?" Joe nodded again at Mrs. Calhoun's question. "I thought so. I'm also assuming that you've never applied for a job with Max Ford. Nor have you any intentions of doing so. At least I hope not. That man stinks of being a cheater and a liar."

"No. I have never wanted to work for anyone but Noah. I'm his day walker. And have been for many decades." She watched their faces. "We have spoken of.... He will be moving along soon anyway, and when he does, I shall be going with him. But he comes here now to speak to you. He does want me to tell you that he will be here soon and that he wishes for you not to be upset with him."

"If he's an enemy of Fords, then he's a friend of ours." Joe said nothing. Noah didn't make friends easily, and he seldom had enemies. If he did, they didn't last long on this earth. He dealt with men who tried to harm him and his just as he did most things...swiftly and without any regret. And Max had made himself an enemy of her boss. "When will he arrive?"

"I have." They all turned to the doorway and Noah smiled at them, not even bothering to hide his fangs as he usually did. "The Calhouns. I have heard a great many things about your pack. It is my pleasure to finally meet you."

CHAPTER 2

Trent tried to focus on what the doctor was telling him, but for the most part his mind was stuck on two words: heart attack. He'd had a mild heart attack, and he would have more if he didn't turn his life around, and soon. He looked at his dad when he snapped his fingers in front of his face.

"He's talking to you. Are you listening?" Nodding, Trent looked back at the doctor. He still didn't have a clue what he was talking about, so he looked at his dad again. "He's telling you how lucky you were that someone was there that could help you. Been up to any of us standing around with our thumbs up our collective bottoms, you'd be a goner about now. He was just telling you what sort of changes you're gonna make or you'll be dead. And you will make changes, boy, or so help me...I can't do that again."

"Mr. Calhoun, I never said that. All I was saying was had he not have the proper care right when it happened, he'd be in worse shape than he is."

Trent nodded. He knew that much. Someone had performed CPR on him when his heart had been in an irregular rhythm. And by them doing that, he'd been able to live, keep oxygen to his brain and his heart pumping like it should have been. Trent looked at the doctor and wondered if the man would just shut up a moment and let his mind grasp what had been said to him.

"Trent?" He looked at the doctor, just realizing that he might have closed his eyes for a moment. They were giving him something powerful, he had to admit that. Usually, meds didn't even faze his kind. "Trent, I need to talk to you about this. I sent your father away for a moment so we could talk."

"He can be a little much." Doctor Sawyer nodded and smiled. "Am I going to be all right? I mean, right now I feel sort of loopy if you want to know the truth."

"We're giving you some pretty heavy doses to keep you calm. You don't have a lot of that in your life, do you, son?" He told him that he'd been trying to keep himself in shape. "That's not what I mean. You're fit and in good shape basically, but not your mind or heart. You need to...I was going to say relax, but it's more than that. You need to talk. To someone that isn't a family member. Blow off steam to someone you can trust. Run as your wolf when you need to. Get out of the office more than you do. Go out on a date."

"You mean get laid." The doctor smiled. "My father. He said something like that to me the other day. I'm not sure he's the right man to suggest something like that, but he did. He's only been with my mom forever. He doesn't understand how hard it is out there for a man like me to date."

Dating and going out with a woman for the sole purpose of getting laid wasn't the same thing. Dating meant you liked the woman; at least that's the way he equated it. You took her to dinner, a movie, or even something as simple as a boat ride. The kind of women he usually went out with wanted no more to do with marriage and long-term relationships than he did. Trent wanted it, wanted it all, but he'd been working too hard to even think about that lately.

"No, I would imagine that it's not. But you need to. Not just to get laid, as you said, but to get away from work. Go fishing with someone. Where there is no cell service. Let your wolf have more time in the woods. Regain that feeling of being one with nature. You've lost that along the way of becoming a great man." Trent started to tell him that he and his wolf were just fine, but the doc looked around the room with a quirked brow. "Don't bother telling me that you've got this, Trent. You just had a minor heart attack at thirty-three. You don't have shit together but your business, and that's killing you."

The doctor stood up and moved toward the door. Trent lay there for several seconds before he called him back. "Am I really going to be all right now? If I get my ass together and do what you say, will I be okay?"

"Yes. But you have to make some major life changes, Trent. Starting today. No more eating what you please. I'm to understand that you had nearly a dozen biscuits before this happened?" Trent nodded, embarrassed. "You can eat what you want *in moderation*. And if you have fun, you can do more of that sort of thing. *In moderation*. You do remember what that is, don't you? Fun, I mean? When was the last time you went on a vacation? Not a business trip where you ate at restaurants because it was convenient, and slept poorly in a hotel. A vacation where you did site seeing, ate at some place you might have read the menu over first. Went to a museum because you wanted to."

"I don't remember." He nodded at him. Trent didn't think he understood. "I just bought a house. Increased our business by nearly triple, and took on two companies that I'm going to have to walk away from because I don't trust the man at the other end. That's a lot of leg work."

"Do you have people working for you?" Trent told him that he had a few hundred. "And they can't do this for you? They can't take over some of the stress and strain for you? If you don't delegate, Trent, you're going to be pushing up flowers and out of work permanently."

He lay there for a long time after he was left alone, just thinking about everything and nothing at all. Trent didn't delegate, not even to his own brother, who had been begging him for more involvement in the business since he'd partnered with him. Trent even did his own payroll, when he knew there were companies out there that could do it in half the time and for very little cost when compared to how much time he spent on it. He was, in a word, stupid.

Someone came into the room a few minutes later. Trent had closed his eyes and didn't look up when the person cleared their throat. It was a female, that he knew, and that she smelled of medicine. When she touched his arm he felt her warm fingers as she grazed them over his elbow, but he still didn't look.

"They just checked my blood pressure a few minutes ago." Nothing. Opening one eye, he looked at the woman standing just a few feet away from the bed and realized his mistake. Sitting up in the bed and looking at her, his first thought was that she was gorgeous. The second was to wonder who she was there for, because he was a lucky guy. "I thought you were a nurse. Is there something I can help you with?"

"Your father sent me to see you." He nodded, wondering what his dad was up to now as she stepped closer to him. "He said that I should introduce myself."

Her scent made his wolf snarl at him. When he moved along his skin, tearing at him, Trent only had a moment to try and control him before the woman took two steps back. His wolf snarled at him again, and Trent tried to calm him. The women turned to the door, her face full of fear, and Trent leapt from the bed to stop her. She was his was all he could think about.

Before he could touch her, or whatever he intended to do, he found himself lifted up by his neck and his airway being cut off. The huge fucking vampire in front of him looked ready to tear his throat out when he snarled at the girl to run. The door opening and closing had his wolf nearly take him.

"My mate." The man stared at him for several seconds before he lowered him to the floor. He didn't let go of him just yet, but his talons were no longer biting into his skin. "She's my mate. I have to get her."

"You'll do no such thing." The sharp shake had Trent fighting dizziness, but then he was let go. Staggering, he nearly fell, then was lifted up and laid in the bed by the vampire. "You frightened her, and she called to me. In all my years of being with her, she has never had a reason to call out to me in fear."

"I need to touch her." Trent didn't just need to touch her…he had to or he'd die. And the need was making him hurt. Then he looked at the man and thought for a second. "She.... My dad did this, didn't he? Sent her in here and made me think she was.... This is some sort of joke, isn't it? She's not really my mate, and someone is just playing tricks on me again."

"I don't think she would find this funny. Do you?" Probably not, but he didn't say that to the vampire. "Noah Stark, at your service. And if she is your mate, you will have a great many things to explain to her. Me as well, but more importantly her. I love her, you see, and I will not see her harmed. Not again, and certainly not by a man that thinks to claim her."

~~~

Christine had no idea what had happened to her son since he was released from the hospital, but she was sure that whatever it was, she could fix it. She loved her sons more than she did her own life and hated to see one of them like this. Sad, lonely...depressed. Even having his favorite things made for him didn't seem to make him come out of it. When TJ, her husband of nearly forty years, came into the office with her, she knew that he had seen it too.

"The doctor told him to take on a new life or die." Christine knew this as well. And she thought that her husband might want to do the same. Well, "want" might have been the wrong word, but he needed to take some precautions as well. She could not live without him either. "He's moping around like he's lost everything. I don't know what to do for him."

"He needs to go home." That much was apparent. He was her son, and she loved him to death, but he needed to go home and begin whatever he was supposed to be doing. And away from her too, she realized. "I can't help him...well, I can, but I think that's not doing him a bit of good. He needs to make his own way in this. We can't do it for him."

"I think you might be right." She was always right, but didn't point that out to her husband just now. It was a joke between the two of them and had been for some time. "He needs a good talking to first. When you going to do that?"

"Me?" TJ nodded. "I see. And this talk, will it be along the lines of him getting his ass in gear and getting out of our house? Or did you want me to be harsh with him?"

"Just get his dander up a little. You can do that. All he does is look at me like I'm not even there. I don't like that." No, Christine thought, her husband would not like being ignored. "You suppose he might need me to set him up again?"

"You do and I will leave you." She knew what TJ had done in hiring a date for Trent. He swore to her that he'd had no idea, but she wondered. While she loved her husband, she worried about where his mind was at times. "I'll talk to him and then we'll go from there. He needs to get on, not sit around here where I'm waiting on him hand over foot."

Christine made her way to the deck, where her son was currently sitting, after asking Meggie to make him a sandwich. She'd missed the young girl, Joe, a great deal the last few days, wondering if her being there might have brought her son out of his funk. Just someone to talk to or to argue with. Christine didn't care at this point.

Trent had been on the deck off and on since he'd come home from the hospital three days ago, and she wondered if he was going to move back in with them. He couldn't. Not now. The doctor had told them that he needed to move, do things for himself. And living with them wouldn't get that for him. As soon as she sat down, Trent started talking.

"He said that he loves her. I'm not sure what I should do now." Before she could ask him who or what he was talking about, he continued. "I had no idea what to think when my wolf recognized her before I did, so I scared her.

And she called for Noah. Now she's gone and he's pissed off and in love with my mate."

"Joe? Joe Samuels is your mate?" He nodded without looking at her. "Trent, are you sure? Well, that's a silly question, of course you are. That's the reason for the long face and moping around here, I take it?"

"She and Noah are leaving soon. If they haven't already. Max Ford is giving him some trouble, so they have to move before he hurts them. He wouldn't...Noah wouldn't give me much in the way of information about her because he said that was up to me." Christine stood up and walked to stand in front of her son. Telling him to stand, she slapped him hard across the face. "What the hell was that for?"

"Did he say he was in love with her or that he loved her?" Without waiting for him to answer, she did for him. "He loves her. Like I do you...most of the time anyway. Right now I want to turn you over my knee and paddle you but good. And don't you think I can't do it either. Noah and Joe, the two of them have been together for decades, he told us that. And here you sit on your bottom, acting like...well, I'm not sure what you're acting like. A spoiled child perhaps? Maybe a baby who's not had a nap? A wolf gets one shot at this, and you're letting it slip through your fingers like it's nothing. Or is it nothing to you?"

"I don't know what this is." He sat back down. "I thought Dad had set it up. And before you hit me again, you know that I have good reason to think that. The man is positively insane to keep me between the sheets for some reason. And then Sawyer comes in and tells me that I need to get out more. Date and see the world with other people. Women, he meant. I was thinking about that, really I was, about how I've not had a vacation in ten years. I don't even enjoy going on business trips because I'm there for as little time as possible. I don't delegate, either, but do it all myself, even ignoring the pleas of my partner, my own brother who I trust with my life to take on more. Then this beautiful woman comes in and I scare the crap out of her by letting my wolf rule my head. To be honest, Mom, I'm thinking that she might be better off without me."

"Why?" He looked at her then, and it twisted up her heart to see him like this. Broken, she thought. Her son was broken. "Trent, why do you think this girl would be better off not loving you?"

"I'm not a nice person. I don't know how to be friendly. I have no friends to speak of but family. And most of the time, I'm sure you want to bash my head in. Or slap me around a bit." He winked at her and smiled. "She had Dad eating out of her hand in only a few days, and a vampire that risked coming out in the sunlight to save her. I don't know how to be that person she needs."

"Oh Trent, what the hell are you thinking?" He looked at her, and she wanted to hit him and hug him at the same time. "As your mother I hate to say this to you when you're down like this, but get up off your ass and fix this. I don't care if you have to hire friends to figure this out. Go to this girl on your hands and knees, but you fix this with her. You will never get another chance at happiness if you don't go and find her."

She stood up, and so did he. When he looked like he was going to say something she put up her hands. It was time to cut the strings with him, and no better way to do that than to simply cut them.

"You have two hours to get your things and move back to your own home. I'm not going to be picking up the pieces when this all hits the fan. Go and sulk or whatever it is you're currently doing to find your mate away from me. Or don't find her." She turned her back on him to go into the house, her heart breaking with each word. "I didn't raise you to be a coward. And from where I'm standing, not only are you that, but you are wasting your life too."

As soon as she entered her house, she turned to the stairs and ran up them to her bedroom. Closing the door behind her, she leaned heavily against it and let the tears fall. Christine knew as surely as she was standing there that she'd done the best thing for her son, but it didn't lessen the pain of it.

An hour later, feeling no better about what she'd done, Christine went to see if he had left. TJ was standing at the bottom of the stairs waiting for her, and she was worried that something had happened. When he slammed his hand down on the banister and told her he was mad at her, she paused in mid-step and waited.

"You ran him off." She pointed out that he'd told her to. "Yeah, I did, but not by telling him that he wasn't welcome here. You know how mad he was when he left here? Powerful, let me tell you."

"Did he tell you that Joe is his mate?" That shut him up. "I see. So all you know is that he left here mad and not any of the details. Well, Trent James Calhoun the fifth, I'm not going to stand for you treating me this way. You have less time than your son had to get out of my house. Leave here right now."

"You're kicking me out of my own house?" She told him she was kicking him out of her life too. "You can't do that. I'm your mate. You can't...what do you think you're doing?"

"What I need to." She walked down the steps and to the door. After opening it, she looked at her husband. "Get out of here before I hurt you. And you know that I will too."

"Honey…Christine, you don't—"

"Don't you dare honey me, you overbearing jackass. I did what I thought needed to be done. I came down here for support, after doing what we talked about. You hear one thing from our son, one small part of what we talked about, and you get mad at me. Well, I got news for you, I slapped him too. You want to do that to me as well?" He told her that he'd never hit her. "No, but you'll hurt my heart without any provocation, won't you? Get out of here, TJ. I don't want to see you right now."

As soon as he left, still trying to sweet talk her, she went to her office and sat behind her desk. Christine had no idea what she was supposed to do now, but she knew that she wasn't going to be pushed around. Reaching for a tissue, she wiped at the tears just as her cell phone rang. Right now she didn't want to talk to any of them and turned her ringer off when it stopped. Then for good measure, she turned the entire phone off.

"Stupid men. I wish we'd had all girls now." Looking at the last family picture that had been taken of them all, Christine stuck her tongue out at it. Crying harder now, she turned her back on the picture and everything else that she had to do today and felt sorry for herself. It was something that she rarely did. "Like that's going to solve a damned thing."

The laugher made her turn and then stand. The man standing there hadn't been invited in, and she wasn't sure what he wanted. "Can I help you?"

"There is no need for you to worry, my dear lady. I have not invaded your home; I could never do that anyway. I am here to speak to you about our children. Joe is…she is

43

very upset with me, and your son, I'm afraid, has hurt her. Perhaps unintentionally, but he has all the same."

"Your child? You mean Joe. I guess...all right, you only think of her as your child. I'm sorry, I'm a little upset at the moment. Also you should know, my son isn't any happier with me. I have resorted to violence, and I'm not proud of myself over it." He laughed again. "I don't think this is the least bit funny. And how is it you're here if you say you've not invaded my home?"

"I am but an image that I can project where I need to be. It is still bright in the day for me, but I wanted to speak to you on Joe's...well, not her behalf, but here I am for her. I fear that if she knew that I was here, she would be a great deal madder at me than she is now. I have pointed out that you have but one chance in life to find your other half, and she is wasting it by hiding out with me." Christine told him she'd said the same to her son. "Ah, so we are thinking alike. I knew that you were a brilliant woman."

Christine wasn't sure about that. She had thrown out her mate too. "What is it you think we can do? And just so we're on the same page here, I'm not going to shove them in the same room and hope they come out on top of this."

"My dear, that is precisely what we must do. The nature of the beast, so to speak, is for him to claim his mate. What better way to have that happen than to toss her to the wolf?" She sat back down at her desk and thought about what he was proposing for them to do. "Joe is ready to leave when I do, if I do. But now that she'll be living here for the long term, I've changed my mind. I have told her, and this was just an idea that I had dancing around in my head, that I had to think about things. I would like to finish this with Mr. Ford. He has become somewhat of a nuisance to me and my household. But short of killing him, which might happen anyway, I need to make sure that he does not follow me to the next place, nor does he hurt my Joe."

"Trent said you told him you loved her." He said that he did. "Love her, or are you *in love* with her?"

"At one time, many years ago, I thought to take her as my own, change her into what I am so that I might have someone to call mine. But as the years went by and her loyalty to me grew, I knew that the only thing that I could do for her was to keep her safe. Changing her into a monster, such as I am, would not have served any purpose but to stem my loneliness. But she has kept that at bay simply by being who she is. So I have taken her into my heart, but only as a father would a child." He smiled at her, and Christine thought it the saddest thing she'd seen, even more so than her own son's sadness. "She saved my life and that of another man even though she cared for neither of us. Offered up her life giving blood to save me after begging for a man that was killed soon after when another wanted the scraps that he'd pulled from the trash. So yes, I do love her, and might be just a little in love with her, but not the way I think that your young Trent can love her."

"I'll do it." Nodding and feeling good about this now, she asked him what she had to do. "I can't hurt them, neither of them. Joe has come to mean a great deal to me, and Trent is my baby boy. I know that he's far from being a child, but he is mine."

"I understand that more than you can know, my dear lady. But all that we need to do is get them together. I'm sure that nature will do the rest." Christine hoped so. She wanted her son happy. "Now. We must think where to lock them in. It should only be for a small amount of time. A few hours at most."

"Trent needs to take a vacation, doctor's orders, and I know just the place he needs to go. There is a lovely cabin just up the mountain on our property. I can have it readied for them in a couple of days. You can tell Joe that you want her to hide out from this Ford person. She'll do that, won't she?' Noah said that she would, for him. "Good. I'll start on that now. I'll let you know when I'm ready. I'll tell him that he has to remain there for a week. He'll do it. He needs to suck up a little to get back in my good graces. I think this will work. I really do."

So it began. When Noah left her, Christine thought that she had to do one more thing before she got the house ready. And that was to make up to her mate. She'd treated him terribly, and she knew it. Reaching out to him, Christine started crying.

I'm so terribly sorry. I love you with all my heart, and I'm so sorry. He told her he was as well. *I love you. And right now I need your help with Trent and Joe.*

Anything, love. Anything you need. She hoped so. What they were about to do was terrible but necessary. *Can I come home now? I'm so sorry for what I said to you. You were right, as usual, and that is what gets me all riled up. I'm so sorry.*

CHAPTER 3

"I'll be back in two days to hang out with you. In the meantime, you're to take it easy and not do much more than just fish and chop wood if you want." Trent nodded at his brother. Sterling had told him he'd bring him up here, but he couldn't stay until the weekend…not that he didn't want to, but could not just yet. The weekend was three days away. But Trent had to do this. It was the only way that his mom would forgive him. "You don't have your cell on you, do you?"

"No. I had to leave it with Mom." That was another thing that he had to do. One day a week he had to turn off his cell phone and his computer and not use them at all. He thought perhaps that was going to be the hardest. "I don't want to die, Sterl. I came close. If this is what I need to do to make myself take it easy, I can do this. Besides, Mom was pretty pissed at me the other day, and I need to make her happy."

"Yeah, she was. Don't ever do that again, okay? Nor are you allowed to have another heart attack. No matter how minor. You scared the shit out of all of us." Trent told him that he wasn't planning on it. "When I come up, I'll bring us some food, along with a few beers. We'll hang out, catch a few fish, and then be better men for it. I'll read up on how to bait our hooks."

Trent didn't even know how to fish. He'd had to look it up on the Internet yesterday when his mom told him what he had to do here. He looked down at the camera—a real one—and wondered if she'd believe him if he told her that it didn't work. To have to take pictures of his fish when he caught them was going to be difficult, because he was sure he was never going to catch any.

When they were boys, their dad had brought them up here to relax, but Trent had never really thought of it as a place to relax. There was always something that had to be done. Wood to chop, though they never seemed to burn it. Branches needed to be picked up. Again, there seemed to be no use for them. And then there was the added bonus that the place had no television or radio. At least indoor plumbing had been added when he was about five, and there was power to the house. He'd hated it from the very beginning. But he now knew that he had missed the point of the venture with his dad and brothers.

Only after they stopped making the trip did he get why they did it. His dad, not much of an outdoorsman either, had wanted them to do things together. Manly things, he guessed. But all it had ever done was make them dread it. Much like he was dreading this now. But he also knew that he had to let things go...rest. And the only way he might be able to do that was to simply get away from it all. And though he didn't want to be here, it was the best place for him.

Trent was actually looking forward to having no phone service. Also the lack of television. What he wasn't going to enjoy was that he was the only one around for miles. He was terrified that he'd have another attack and no one would be there to help him. His mother told him he would be fine. Trent wasn't so sure. Sometimes in the middle of the night he'd wake, feeling the pain in his chest so badly he thought for sure it was happening again.

After they unloaded the truck of his clothing and the food that he'd had to bring, Sterl sat on the front part of the wrap-around porch with him as the sun went down. It would be pitch black out soon, and Trent was sort of worried for his brother driving in it. Not that he couldn't handle it, but he still worried about him. Trent seemed to worry about a great many things concerning the wellbeing of his family these days.

At a little after ten, his brother said he had to go. "You call to me if you need me. I'll be here as quickly as I can." Trent told him he would. "You're going to be fine, Trent. Mom just wants you to take it easy for a little while. Hell, we all might have to take turns if this works out for you."

"You never know. You might come back and I'll have decided to live here." Not likely, but Sterl laughed. "Be careful."

When he was alone—and out here he really was alone—Trent sat back on the porch and looked out over the lake. It was a beautiful place, and the real sounds of nature beat the canned experience on the CDs he'd recently been listening to. They were said to help you relax. Trent had wanted to break the CD after ten minutes.

The place had been his parents' home when they had first married. Back then it had been one bedroom with a large living, kitchen, and dining area all in one. An outhouse had been out back, and there had been no running water or power. But that had all changed recently.

Trent had known that his parents had made some updates, but he'd not known how extensive they were until now. It was as good if not better than the home he'd just bought. And a good deal bigger. It was huge now, even by cabin standards.

There were eight big bedrooms, each with their own bathroom, a large eat in kitchen, plumbing, and running water to the entire house and some places out on the beautiful deck. The living room boasted a large fireplace and air conditioning for the hot hazy days of summer. The deep freeze, according to his mom, was full, and the walk-in pantry was fully stocked. He did wonder how long she expected him to stay.

The place was set for him to live here for the rest of the summer should he want to, but he didn't think it would come to that. He really did have some things that he needed to take care of in town, but in order to make his mom happy, he was here for ten days. Ten long and lonely days, not counting when Sterl came to see him.

Going in around midnight after watching the deer roam around for a bit and hearing every sound that was made in the woods beyond, he made his way to the master bedroom. It had, according to his mom, the nicest mattress. He decided to take a long, hot shower and hope that it would relax him enough that he'd be able to sleep. Sleep wasn't his best friend of late.

His business was hurting a little from the sting of walking away from Ford Enterprises. Not anything that they'd not recover from; billing hours mostly. But he knew now that his brother had been right. He'd come to learn that Elijah knew a great deal about business, and had he turned to him at any point, they might have been able to foresee the issues with Ford before it had all gone to shit.

That was on his list of new Trent laws…listen to his family and let them do more for him. Even at the risk of driving him crazy.

Pulling a towel from the rack, Trent simply dried himself off as he made his way to his cases that were on the bed, not bothering with the soft pants and boxers he'd brought into the bathroom with him. But the sight of Joe in his room had him holding the towel tightly in front of his naked body.

"I think there's been a mistake." Not as far as Trent could see, but he said nothing to her. "I was told that I could hide out here and not have to worry about Mr. Ford trying to hurt me. I don't think anyone knew you were going to be here."

"He won't. Ford will never touch you again so long as I'm alive." His voice sounded thicker even to him. "I was taking a shower. I didn't hear you come in."

"I should leave." Trent took a step toward her and she took one back. "I don't want to be here with you. You…I have no more use for you than you do me. It was a mistake, my coming here."

"I'm sorry about the other day." She didn't move when he took another step toward her. Trent tightened his grip on the towel when he felt his cock hardening beneath it. "It was never my intention to frighten you like I did. I only wanted to touch you. My wolf, he can be a little aggressive when he sees something that he wants."

"You should back up." He didn't, but took two more steps toward her. She moved back, and when her back hit the door behind her, Trent closed the distance between them. "Don't touch me, Mr. Calhoun. I'm not what you think I am. I'm not even sure you didn't have it right when you said we'd been set up."

"My mate. That's who you are and no one, not even my father, could have tricked me into that." He ran his fingers down her cheek with his free hand and thought there wasn't anything softer than her skin. "My wolf scared you, didn't he? When he recognized you as our mate, he scared you. I'm sorry about that."

"He did no such thing." He nearly smiled at the indignant sound in her voice but didn't. She licked her lips then, and he watched in fascination as her moist tongue traced along the very flesh he wanted to taste. "You're too close to me. Could you please back away? We can talk in the other room, but not here."

"Why not here?" Trent leaned down to her mouth and brushed his lips over hers before taking her lower lip into his mouth and nipping at it. "Is it because this is the bedroom? Or that I'm naked here in this room with you? Am I scaring you now, Joe? Do you want to run from me again? If you do, then my wolf is going to take me and I'm going to let him run you down. He'd like that, to chase his mate and tear your clothing off to taste you."

She was aroused. He could smell it, and his wolf was as thrilled as he was about it. She moaned slightly when he touched his fingers to her throat then down over her shoulder. Trent wanted to take her now, against this wall, only to toss her to the bed and take her there too. But he also knew that he didn't want to scare her again. Never again.

"You need to back away from me now." Her hand touched his arm, and he felt her heat. When her fingers curled around his arm, as if to hold onto him, he leaned in and took another taste of her lips. "This is going much too fast for me. I know nothing about you."

Instead of answering her, even if he could have, he dropped his towel and let it fall to the floor between them. As he lifted her up by cupping her ass, her legs wrapped around his hips. Her body molded against his like she'd been made to fit there, which, in a way, she had been.

He needed her. Wanted to mark her as his mate, make love to her until he couldn't move. But he didn't want to hurt her, and possibly scare her into not trusting him. He rocked into her heat, feeling her need as she rolled her hips toward his. Moving his mouth along her throat to her pounding pulse, he nipped her there.

She came then, her body holding his tightly in her grip as she cried out her release. Pulling her to his body, he made his way to the bed and laid her over it. His cock was tight with the need to release. Precum dripped from the tip, and he fisted his cock so he could get a grip on himself. But when she sat up, her body still clothed, Trent nearly cried out when she licked his crown and held him in her mouth.

"I want to see you." Nodding, she lay back on the bed and started to unbutton her blouse. "Now, baby. I need you now."

Pulling her from the bed, he staggered slightly when her weight fell against his. Trent loved having her body close to his, and kissed her again while he reached to the bottom of her blouse and ripped it from her. Next were her pants. Sliding his hand down into the top of them, he gripped the material hard, trying not to think about how her ass was right there for him, and tore them from her as well. When she stood in only her panties and bra, he took a step back.

"Christ." She was more beautiful than he'd ever imagined. And over the last several days he'd imagined her a great many ways. When she cupped her breasts, her nipples spilling from the top of the bra, he knew that if she touched him now he was as good as dead.

"I've never had sex before. I've thought of it often." He nodded, watching as she played with her breasts. When they were naked, the bra shoved up over them, he whimpered when he saw her thick nipples, hard as stone, being tugged on by her hands. "I've given myself pleasure before. I love coming, don't you?"

"You're killing me. Let me see all of you." She nodded and pulled her bra off and dropped it to the floor. "Panties. Please, take them off before I do it for you."

"I don't know why I want you so badly, do you?" He told her again that she was his mate, his other half. Trent wasn't sure if he was making sense, but he was watching her fingers dance down the front of her body. "Will you give me pleasure too?"

"Yes. As much as you want." When she bent at the waist and stood up, her last barrier to him gone, he dropped to his knees in front of her. "I'm going to drink from you. I can smell how aroused you are, and all I can think of doing is eating you."

Not waiting for an answer, he pulled her to him and his mouth. As soon as he took her clit in his mouth, he bit down, bringing her to a quick climax. Trent was going to feast on her, even if it killed him. And right now, he didn't care if he died…he had his mate.

~~~

Joe wasn't sure what she had expected when he brought her body to his mouth. She knew what oral sex was…she'd have to be stupid to have not heard of it over her lifetimes. But what he was doing to her body right now bordered on ecstasy. More than that, it had to be the best thing she'd ever experienced. When she came twice more, his mouth eating her as if she were a fine steak, she felt her knees weaken each time. Trent backed her up, using his mouth and hands, and Joe fell onto the bed. Looking up at him as he knelt between her thighs, she thought perhaps he was the most beautiful thing she'd ever seen.

He moved closer to her, his fingers spreading her nether lips open as his mouth descended to her. When he suckled her clit into his mouth, she watched him, riding his mouth as he brought her to peak again. When he lifted his head from her, just enough that she could see his mouth, she wanted to beg him not to stop, but he slid his fingers over her clit again and spoke.

"I'm going to stretch you for my cock." Nodding, she wondered aloud if it would hurt. "No. I hope not anyway. But I plan to eat you until you're so ready for me that you won't care if there is a little pain with it."

"I'm ready for you now." He shook his head and fucked her with his fingers. "I like that. Very much. More. I need more."

He fucked her this way, his mouth devouring her as his fingers moved in and out of her faster and faster. She never came again; it was wonderful, but as soon as she was ready to release he'd pull back and start anew. Joe was ready to hit him when he stood up over her.

His cock was thicker than it had been before. Longer too, she thought. Sitting up, she reached for him only to have him step back. He told her if she touched him, he'd come now instead of inside of her.

"I want to be there when I come, deep inside of you. Feeling you tightening around me as you come." She wanted that as well and lay back when he told her too. Opening her legs felt strange, but she was so needy by now that she would have done most anything for some sort of

55

relief. As he joined her on the bed, pulling her to the middle where he was, she felt her body tense up again.

"No, love, don't. I just want to taste these lovely breasts now." He leaned over her and took just her nipple into his mouth and nibbled. She rose up, curling her fingers in his hair in hopes of him giving her something more. But the harder she tried to get him to touch her again, the more he pulled back. Finally, she rolled him to his back and sat over him. His cock was just between her nether lips, and she ran her finger over the crown that was dark and full of blood.

"I want to feel you now. I need to have you inside of me so that I can come again." He nodded and helped her sit up on her knees. As he held his cock in his hand he told her to lower herself over him slowly so as not to hurt either of them. She leaned on his chest and watched as her pussy seemed to eat his cock. It was erotic seeing him like this, and she felt him fill her up even as she knew it was hurting him to be so gentle with her.

"Slowly love. Please, go slowly." She moved her hips, trying her best to feel every inch of him. But when he moaned, she stopped and looked at his face. He was in a great deal of pain, she thought. "I'm trying not to slam you down over me. I want to take you hard and fast, but I know that it'll hurt."

Moving her hips again, she watched his face. Yes, he was in pain, but not the kind from a wound…he was in pain from trying to keep her safe. Moving her hips once more, she took a deep breath and moved downward, impaling herself over him. The pain of it took her breath away and she couldn't hold back the scream that spilled from her throat. Stilling herself over him, wondering why she ever thought this would be good, Joe wanted to lift her body off his and move back to Noah.

Joe realized that he was speaking to her. She didn't know what he was saying, but he was talking in low soothing tones as he held her. His cock was still inside of her, deep and painfully so, but when she moved, just enough to try and dislodge him, the pain was replaced by the most incredible pleasure. His hand at her ass stopped her from moving again.

"Don't move just yet, baby. Please?" Nodding, she moved again anyway. "Christ, you're killing me. I want to fuck you but I know that you hurt."

Moving her hips again, she felt his cock fill her again. When he rolled her to her back, his body between her legs, she lifted them up and wrapped her feet over his thighs. As he moved, slowly at first then with more power and speed, all Joe could think about was there was something there, just out of her reach, and he was keeping it from her.

"I'm going to bite you." Yes, she told him, and tilted her head so that he could. She had no idea how, but she knew that his bite, his teeth taking her flesh, was going to be much better than the few times that Noah had bitten her. "Christ baby, I'm going to come if you keep this up. I need to fill you. Mark you."

As soon as his teeth grazed her throat, she came. It was as if that was all she had been waiting for. And when he bit her, tore into her throat, Joe came again, screaming out her release as if it were coming from the bottom of her feet. Biting him on the shoulder to try and stem the feelings that were washing over her, she tasted his blood as it bubbled up on his skin.

Nothing could have prepared her for the immediate and profound connection. His thoughts were hers, his need filled her. Even his need to keep her from hurting too much touched her mind. And when he bowed up from her, his mouth still stained red from her own blood, she watched as he threw back his head and howled, his wolf racing along his skin, which touched off another powerful climax in her.

Joe felt the tug of darkness as he filled her again, his body pounding hard against hers, his cock filling her in a way that she knew no one ever would again. And when he held her to his throat, she did what seemed as natural to her as breathing and bit down on his pulse, tasting his blood as it not only filled her mouth, but her every fiber as well. It was all it took to take her over the edge again and into the abyss of darkness.

When she woke she was alone in the big bed. Stretching, she tried to tell herself that she'd been stupid for doing this with the man, but she felt much too good to listen to her head at the moment. When she heard him whistling she realized that she might come to enjoy living here with him, if only for a little while, and got up to find something to wear. As she was searching for her panties, she saw him standing in the doorway.

"Seems a shame to cover all that beauty up. But I'm sure that you're as hungry as I am." Nodding, suddenly embarrassed, she covered her body with the shirt she'd unearthed only moments ago. "Are you sore? I can run you a bath if you want. We're having chops on the grill, but I can take them off if you need a bath first."

"I can eat first." Nodding, he didn't move. "I didn't know that you were going to be here. I was told that I could stay here without any trouble."

"I've been thinking about that as I made us some dinner. I think we've been set up. I'm not sure yet by who, but I'd bet that either my dad or mom did this. Noah too, I would guess." She hadn't thought of that, them being thrown together on purpose. "Come into the kitchen when you're ready. I have things just about done, and we'll talk there."

Joe thought about calling out to Noah to find out if he had done this to her. She was just mad enough at him to leave him to his own devices. But she wanted to talk to Trent first; he might have already spoken to him. Not like she was going to, but she would give him a piece of her mind when she did. Pulling on her clothing, she made her way to the kitchen to find the table set for two and fresh flowers in a pretty pottery vase in the middle of the table.

"They're for you. I went out and picked them...it's kinda dark out, so if some of them are weeds and not flowers, that's what I'm blaming it on." Nodding, she sat down when he pulled out her chair for her. "I wasn't sure what kind of vegetables you ate, so I made a variety of them. I can cook a little, mostly the simple things, but I wanted to make this special for you."

"Why?" She flushed when she realized that she'd spoken aloud. "I'm sorry. I just don't understand how you can be like this when we've been played. And we were, weren't we? Played like we have no sense to come in out of the rain."

He put two chops on her plate and handed her a bowl that had peas, carrots, and corn all in different places inside of it. She watched him pull rolls out of the oven and bring those, as well as two glasses of tea, to the table. When he sat down, she stared at all the food, then at him.

"I know, it's a lot of food. But I've been in a funk and this is the first time I've felt hungry in a while." Nodding, she watched him pick up his first pork chop and eat it like one would an ear of corn. "As for us being played. I really can't find that I'm mad at anyone over it. I had messed up with you, badly, and I was feeling sorry for myself at my mom's home when she kicked me to the curb. This, coming up here, was my way of making it up to her. Or so I thought. I think now that it was a plan all along to get us in the same room. I'm not...I'm sorry that you were put here this way, but I can't be upset about the outcome."

"You said that I was your mate. I know what that means, but I'm not sure what that will entail when I have to leave when Noah does." He told her that she wasn't going anywhere unless he did too. "There is no reason for you to leave your home. I can come to you when you need me."

"I need you all the time. Not just sexually, but in my life." He put down his second chop bone and looked at her. "I want you in my life. I need you there. I haven't felt this good in months...hell, probably years. You're my mate, and while it's nothing we can control, I do want to make you a part of my life. And with that, be a part of yours."

"I'm not human." He grinned at her and told her that he wasn't either. "No, you don't understand. I'm an immortal. I have...Noah made me one when he asked me to be his day walker. I cannot die. You will. This cannot work. You have to see that, Trent. I'm going to live forever. We don't have a lot of time together as mates."

"Yes, it will work, and we have as much time as we can give each other. If we aren't together, I'm not going to be able to live anyway, now that I've found you. And we'll have to put as much living into our lives together until I'm gone. I want you to remember me forever, even after I'm gone." She nodded, not sure he was understanding what she was saying. "I'm not going anywhere, Joe. And I hope that you won't either. We are together in this, even if only one of us is in the 'till death do I' part."

She picked up her knife and fork and thought that what he'd just said wasn't funny. True, but not at all funny.

Biting into the chop, she moaned. Okay, if he cooked like this all the time, she might enjoy this more than she was already.

Chapter 4

Max stood on the front stoop for ten minutes after ringing the doorbell eight times. Wherever the bastard was, he wasn't at home, he realized. And he needed to talk to Trent right now. He wanted him to bail him out like he'd said he would. Moving down the steps to his car, he wondered where the hell the man could be after leaving the hospital, and thought maybe he'd gone to his mother's house.

"I'd be no more welcome there than I have been anywhere else, I'm sure." His driver said nothing when Max spoke his thoughts aloud. The man had been trained not to ever speak or repeat anything he might hear as his driver, or he'd meet the same fate as his predecessor. Death was hard to overcome when you fucked up with him.

As he was driven home again, Max wondered why the deal had been suddenly stopped. He knew that he had covered his tracks well; hell, there were times when he couldn't remember where all the skeletons were in his own closet. But this man had figured out something that had been buried, hidden away or simply killed. Whatever it was, someone was going to pay for that mistake coming to light. Pulling out his little black notebook, he marked when he was at Trent's home and who was with him. He even put that the man didn't appear to be home. For all he knew that man could have been hiding in the hallway just where he couldn't see him. Then there was the matter of Noah Stark.

Noah had fucked with him years ago. Not that he didn't deserve it, but there had been no reason for Noah sticking his nose where it didn't belong. Which was just as Max was going to come into some big money via marrying a bitch that had more money than she did good sense. As was the case for most women he knew. Stupid women were his biggest victory, he thought. Except that one time…but he'd gotten her in the end too.

Max had spent a great deal of money and time on getting not just his appearance changed, but his prints had been burned off and his identity erased as well after that. He wasn't the same person he'd been all those years ago, and had the scars to prove it. Even his weight, which had been well over three hundred pounds, had been shed in an effort to keep Noah from finding him. And now here he was, right in the middle of his biggest money maker yet. Or at least that fucking woman was, and he knew that Joe was a good deal smarter than the average women. Maybe smarter than most men he knew as well. Max had dealt with her before and had come out the loser.

Benson Cartwright, the name he'd been going by back then and his real name, had been stupid. Only in the sense that he'd allowed himself to get caught. The plan had been brilliant and would have worked, had Noah not come upon him and the woman one night when he'd been about to convince her to marry him.

Sydney Carlin had been a hard sell. Harder than any other women he'd scammed before. He had tried his best to be friendly to her, even going so far as to court her, but the kid next door and the stubbornness of the stupid woman had made the deal harder and harder to close. Then Noah had shown up. Max had tried his best to stand between him and his intended, but neither of them seemed to notice him.

"Hello, Sydney. How have you been?" She told him that she'd been great and ignored introducing Max to the man. "I see that Benson has decided to pursue you in the worst kind of way. My dear, I do hope you have hidden away all of your jewels. He's a known rake and thief. Not to mention, he is more than likely a murderer as well."

"To say such a thing. I don't know you from anyone else." Noah said nothing but looked at Sydney. Max tried again to push his way between Sydney and Noah, but he just wasn't having it. "You should really leave us to our business."

But Noah didn't leave, nor did he stop. How he knew anything about Max was beyond him, but he knew and had taken it upon himself to tell Sydney all of it, even his plans for taking her money and her life. And he didn't stop there either.

"Sydney, don't marry this man. He really does mean to take your money and then your life. You would be better off going on and never talking to him, seeing him, or having anything at all to do with this man, period." Noah had glanced at him before looking back at the woman of his dreams, rich and stupid. "In fact, I would tell everyone you know. Spread his name and his picture to every one of your friends. Take out a small advertisement in the paper. Tell everyone what a scoundrel and a cad he is."

She'd done just that. After getting up from the table, leaving him with the bill, Sydney left him sitting there. Then Noah had walked away, laughing. The next day he'd not only been unable to see the woman, but the paper had put out a half page ad about him, including his financial information and that he was preying on others to line his pockets. Max had left in a hurry after women and men started showing up at his door to blast him. Some even threatened to tar and feather him. Max knew that it was all because Noah had told them to do it. Not even the brat next door had given him this much trouble.

But as with many things that he did, Max came out on top, and in a small satisfying way, he'd gotten some of what he'd wanted. Sydney was dead, and no one was none the wiser.

And now here Noah was again, intruding on his business. But there was the added fact that Noah didn't know him. Or anything about this new person he'd come to be. Max thought that he might just have a little fun with the other man and see if he could ruin something for him while he was at it. Maybe even take away the one person that the man seemed to love more than he did anything else. Joe Samuels.

"Sir?" Max looked at the open door to his car and the man's face there. He had no idea how long they'd been stopped, but Max didn't care that the man seemed to be laughing at him. Lifting his foot up, he slammed his booted foot into the man's face and smiled when he stumbled back to the sound of breaking bones. Not even bothering to step over the man, Max made sure that he ground his foot into the softest part of his body as he made his way out of the limo to the house. He'd bet anything that the man would show up to work tomorrow with his face bandaged up, and without a word about what he'd made Max do to him. As soon as he was in the house, he told the butler to have the man fired and his things tossed out with his body first thing. Not waiting for an answer, Max made his way to his office. Things would be done the way he wanted them or there would be hell to pay.

He wasn't surprised to find his phone ringing the moment that he sat down at his desk. Things were progressing now, at least he hoped they were, and they would be finished before he moved on to the last phase of his plan. His plan to be one very wealthy and happy man living as far from here as he could.

"Where the hell have you been? I've been trying to contact you all day." He cocked a brow at the tone of the man on the other end of the phone and didn't bother answering him. The sooner this man was out of his life, the better that would be as well. "Did you see today's paper? What the hell are we going to do now? Huh? Answer me that. You said this was a done deal. It doesn't sound like a done deal to me."

"Perhaps if you gave me some idea as to what I might have missed while trying to line up a meeting with our Mr. Calhoun, then I could answer you." Jefferson Marshall only huffed at him. Pulling his gun from the top desk drawer and laying it on the top of his blotter, Max felt better just knowing that soon this man would feel the bite of his wrath too. "Jefferson, take a breath and tell me what I have missed."

"Trent Calhoun is out of town indefinitely." That certainly wasn't in the plan, but was nothing that couldn't be overcome. He asked him why that was so earth shattering. "Because, according to this morning's paper that you have not even bothered to read, he might be closing down his business. Sources say that he has had enough and won't be opening when he returns, if he even returns. I'm having someone look into seeing if this is true or not. But I'm telling you right now, this will be the end of us if he doesn't help us out of this hole you got us in."

Max tried to slow his mind down to the implications of what this would mean. What could have happened to Calhoun that he'd just forsake all his clients? And he had a great many of them too. Max had done his research on the man and knew that he had money enough to burn. And then some. Something had gotten to him...or someone. Noah Stark. Max thought for sure that Noah was behind this closure.

Max realized that Jefferson was still talking and asked him to please shut up. The silence was so abrupt, he'd thought he'd hung up on him. Jefferson didn't know the half of what was going on with their business. He had no idea that Calhoun had backed out of their deal, and he certainly had no idea that Noah was behind all of it, nor what Calhoun had said to him that day in the office.

"I'm sorry, but we're going to have to decline going into business with you." Max had laughed a little and the younger man only stared at him. "My brother and I have been looking into some of your dealings, and we've found that you're not telling the entire truth, are you? Like for instance, where is the money for the retirement funds for the people that work for you? Also, you haven't paid their insurance premium in months, and the company is going to cut them off soon."

"I don't know where you've found that information, but I assure you, none of it's true. We've been in business for a while now, and we've always kept up with those payments. I'll have to talk to my partner...perhaps he knows." Elijah said nothing, but slid a paper toward Max. Right there in black and white was his name on all the billings, as well as his address. "This can be taken care of when you and your firm bail us out. It's what you do, right?"

"No. We help companies grow…we don't keep them from prison. And we certainly don't get in bed with crooks." Elijah sat down just as the door behind him opened. "Mr. Edwards will show you out, Mr. Ford. Have a good day. And good luck with getting anyone else to loan you any money."

And Elijah had been right. No one else would touch him, not even enough for him to make an appointment to tell them what he needed. He really needed this to work. But he had to get rid of Jefferson for now.

"I'll call you back when I find out what is going on with this. I'm sure that we just have to figure out what their plans are for all of this. We can only hope that it's nothing more than an overzealous reporter with too much time on his hands." It would be just Max's luck if it were true and he'd be out all his money. Noah was going to pay for fucking this up for him. "I'll talk to you tomorrow when I go into the offices. In the meantime, just sit tight and let me handle this."

"Letting you handle things is what got us into this in the first place." Max started to tell the man to fuck off, but didn't get the chance before he spoke again. "You fuck this up, Max, and I swear to you I'll not work with you again." Big threat. He wasn't going to be around to work with anyone.

After he hung up, Max tried to think of what he could do now. He didn't even have enough to leave the country right now. All his money had gone into making a good impression on the stupid dog and to Max's accounting firm overseas. His plan to leave the country with a great deal of ready cash was slowly falling apart. Calhoun had really fucked up his plans in backing out. Max wanted to think of a way to make him come up to the plate with money in hand, or he was going to have to think of more creative ways to get the money from someone else. He wasn't above kidnapping and holding someone for ransom at this point.

"But it wouldn't get me nearly what I want in all of this. And there is the risk of it not working. Then I'll be fucked too." There was money, a great deal of it. Just where he couldn't get to it just now. Max had thought as he was sending his money out that he should have some rainy day money and he'd had a little, but he'd spent it. Lavish dinners, limo drivers, and a few new suits had taken care of that. He had travel expenses to gather, and he wanted to go out with a bang. When he left this country, he was going to make sure that everyone knew that he'd been here.

Max knew that he could call and get money wired to his bank here. And he'd thought of it several times over the last few days. But doing that would be evidence that he had money elsewhere. Not to mention the penalties and fines that he would incur when he did that. Max looked down at his new suit and smiled. Being broke right now had really given him a fine set of clothes.

When his phone rang a little before seven, Max actually thought about not answering it. He was in the middle of making plans, poor ones, but making them all the same, and finally reached for it with a bark of his name. When he was greeted with silence on the other end. It took him several seconds to realize that he might have pissed someone off, like he even cared.

"Mr. Ford?" He felt his balls crawl up into his body. No one had this number but his business partner and his butler. They were the only two that could call him directly. The voice at the other end of the line had a tone that made him think that they'd gone to great links to get the number…and not only that, they had enjoyed it too. "Mr. Max Ford, correct?"

"Yes." Max thought he knew the voice. It was eerily quiet on the other end, but he was pretty sure that Noah was calling him. "Who is this?"

"Oh, I'm sure you've figured it out by now. Please tell me that you've not forgotten our little play time together. I will be very hurt if you have." Max wanted to hang up, but fear made him pull the phone tighter to his ear. "What do you think you're doing, threatening my friends? And lying too. You should know that liars always get what's coming to them. And you are one of the biggest ones I know."

"Look, Noah. I don't know what she told you, but I just wanted to hire her as my…to come and work for me." He had no idea what the woman could do other than predict the market better than most men he knew. But getting her in his home had seemed like a good plan at the time. "I had no idea that she was related to you."

"Then why did you tell her that you were going to need to talk to me? What reason could you think that I'd want a thing to do with any of your business dealings?" Max tried to think what he'd told the woman when he'd seen her on the streets that day and again at the hospital. "Come now, you must have had a reason to have one of your henchmen hold her while you spit on her with your anger. Bad move on your part, that. You do know that I can trace a man through his scent, no matter what he might have done to his physical appearance?"

"What do you mean you can trace someone through their scent?" He was trying to think if he'd ever heard that Noah was a shifter, and hadn't. The man was a recluse and a pain in his ass, but he'd never known anyone to say he was anything but a human. "Did you have someone take my DNA, Noah? Is that what you've done?"

"No, my dear boy. I tasted it. And that alone gives me all kinds of information that most people I know would never have realized about you." Max tried to think what the fuck he was talking about when he spoke again. "Being a vampire affords me all sorts of gifts that you should be finding out about soon enough. But I will tell you right now, I have a memory like a steel trap. You can change your looks, but I know you better than you do yourself."

The laughter echoed in his head long after the man hung up on him. Max laid the phone back in the cradle, and his hands shook. He also felt the beads of sweat as it rolled down his back and pooled at his spine. He was in so much trouble here. More than he would ever thought he'd be in. Noah Stark was a fucking vampire. And he knew everything.

~~~

Trent tried to make the stupid pole work, but all he seemed to be able to catch was the trees around him or some hidden log or weed in the bottom of the lake, just waiting to tangle him up. He looked over at Joe when she laughed. Who would have thought that someone having fun at your expense would make you feel so good?

"You've never done this before, have you?" He shook his head and handed her his pole again. She had a magical touch with it. Every time he was tangled, she just make a few adjustments and he'd be free to get it messed up again. "How could a man that has such a lovely home here not know how to do something as basic as fishing? Not to mention baiting a hook, or even untangling a line when it is just above your head?"

"My dad tried to teach us when we were boys. He'd haul us up here and we'd make a weekend of it. It never was a very good adventure for us. We'd fight and whine and he'd end up coming out here to fish on his own. I think it was simply a way to give my mom a break. She needed it with us. Not to say that she didn't love us, but I would imagine that six boys running full tilt around a house would make any woman a little tense."

He watched her rather than try to cast out again. Twice now he'd had to go out into the warm water and retrieve his pole, and both times she'd stood on the dock and laughed. Tomorrow they were going to go out in the boat. He was terrified to think how that would end. Sure, the water was warm and it felt good on his poor beaten body, but he just knew he was going to tip them and he'd drown her trying to save her. He wasn't the outdoorsman type.

"When Noah and I were on the run, we'd do this for my food. It was less fun then, wondering if I'd be able to get a meal or not." She cast her line in and watched the tiny bobber on the end as she continued. "Then one night while I slept, he went into town and got me some food. I woke the next morning to eggs and other treats that we usually could not have carried with us after we fled his home. It was hard at times, but Noah always took care of me. And I him. Michael has been with us forever, as well as Meggie's relatives. We're all the family we ever needed, I guess."

"I would imagine that you had to run a great deal. Do you still?" She shook her head and smiled at him. "Christ, you're beautiful."

"Thank you, but you're not going to eat if you don't catch something." He nodded and tried his best to imitate what she was doing. "Slowly. Cast it out slowly, remembering that there are trees above you and things lurking beneath that you can catch but not eat. Take your time and think about putting the bobber out there, not above you."

He tried what she suggested and was quite proud of himself when he had not snagged the branches that seemed to jump in his way, or his body. Twice now she'd had to come and cut the line from his arm or his leg. It was most embarrassing to say the least. Keeping his eye on the little red and white ball out further than he'd ever been able to make it go, he spoke to Joe.

"Tell me about your life with Noah. I'm sure it's been an adventure living with a vampire." He wanted to ask her if he'd fed from her, but he was pretty sure that was how she'd saved his life. Noah had told him that he was indebted to Joe more than he could ever repay her. "How long have you lived with him?"

"Nearly eight hundred years." He glanced in her direction when she said that. "Careful. I was about seventeen at the time. I was never sure of my birthdate, but I think that was about right. He was being hurt by a man that I knew. Abraham. He was going to kill him for some of his money. It wasn't much, I don't think, but we were always so hungry. I bargained for their lives."

"And he was killed later. I think Noah mentioned that." She nodded and pulled on her pole. A fat fish nearly leapt up on the shoreline as she reeled it in. She'd be eating well tonight while he was going to have potatoes at this rate. He was really hungry too. Eating smart had a way of not—

"Trent, you have a bite." It took his fuzzed mind a few seconds to register what she'd said to him, and he looked at the ball as it went under again.

He nearly dropped the pole in his excitement. The bobber was nowhere in sight, and the string on his pole was as taut as he'd ever seen it. Reeling it in as he'd seen her do, she told him to set the hook.

This was where he had problems. Setting the hook in the mouth of the fish meant jerking on the line hard enough to make it stick in the fish, yet not pull out so that he would escape. This time he tried for gentle and laughed when the fish took off again, still at the end of his line.

Reeling and pulling was a lot more work than he'd thought it would be. Joe just seemed to bring the fish right in, but he was having to pull and reel over and over. When she went to the water's edge with the net, he knew it was going to be the smallest fish in all the lake despite the fact that he'd been working so hard.

When she laughed, his embarrassment grew until she pulled the net out of the water. He stood there with his mouth open as she turned and laid the net with his catch in it on the bank. He'd caught a monster. His first thought was that she'd blown up a fake fish and put it there for him.

"I think he weighs a bit more than seven pounds." She pulled it from the net like an expert and put it on the small scale that she'd unearthed from the tackle box. It was real, he knew it then, as it flopped and jerked to get away. Trent had no idea what most of the crap in the tackle box was for, but she seemed to know what she was doing. "Oh Trent, he weighs nine pounds, four ounces. Here, hold him so that I can take his picture with you."

She'd been allowed to bring her phone. Not that they'd made much use of the phone itself, but they had taken a great many pictures with it. And last night, after their dinner, she'd pulled out her laptop and they'd downloaded them onto it. After he posed for a half dozen pictures with the fish, he asked to see them.

"I look like a kid." She told him he was to her. "I suppose so. Can you send them to my parents? I was supposed to be up here relaxing and taking pictures of me doing that. She gave me this antiquated camera that I was supposed to use, and then.... Ahh. She knew you were coming. See, this is coming to light more and more. Relax, Trent, she said to me."

"You feel relaxed?" He told her he did. "You do look better than the first time I saw you. I was afraid for you, if you want to know the truth."

She'd told him last night that she had been the one to give him CPR. He might have been told that before, by his dad or doctor, but he didn't remember. But now, even if he had known, it meant more to him.

They fished for a little while longer. He heard her phone go off once or twice, but he never thought to ask her if it was important. Trent found he didn't really care if anyone came to see them again. He'd already contacted his brother and asked him not to come up, and had found out that he'd been wrong about his dad. He'd known about the plan to throw Joe and Trent together, of course, but it had not been solely his plan.

"Mom planned this? I don't believe it. She's not the devious type." Sterl laughed when he did. "I thought I was in deep shit when she told me to get out of the house that day. I guess she knew all along that this is what I needed."

"Apparently. Oh, before I forget to tell you, the paper ran a false story two days ago. About the time you left, as a matter of fact. Anyway, it says that you've closed your doors. Elijah has been working to find out who might have done it. But for now, instead of trying to get a retraction, he's letting it ride. I think he thought it would give you both a much needed break. I guess he thinks it might be the work of that guy, Ford, anyway, a way to get back at you for turning him down." Trent said he could see him doing that. "Whatever happens, he's got it under control, so don't worry about it."

And he hadn't. Not even to worry about whether or not this would hurt his business. Trent was loving every single moment he was up here even if it was under dubious reasons. He looked over at Joe when she said his name.

"This house, does it belong to you or your family?" He told her his parents. "I love it here. Would they sell it to me, you think? I could live up here forever with all the quiet and no neighbors. I know that I have a job, but this is a place I could come and let go."

"Me too. Although when I first came up here, all I could think about was going home again." He moved over to where she was standing and put his arm around her. He'd put his pole away when she said she was tired, and was glad now that his hands were free to do this. Looking out over the lake, he thought about the house he'd just bought and wondered what he'd do with it if his parents would sell the cabin to him and Joe. "I don't have a lot of on-hand cash right now. But I'll ask them. Would you live up here with me?"

"You don't have to worry about money now." He said he rarely did anyway. "What I mean to say is, I have enough for us. We're mates now, and what's mine is yours. I know that much about your kind. I think I like that rule too."

"I don't need your money." He felt her stiffen in his arms and remembered something that had happened between his parents long ago regarding money.

His mom had a great deal when she and dad had first gotten together. She'd inherited it from her family, and his dad had been a little touchy about it. He'd had it in his head that he was the provider, his mom had told him years later, and she'd had to point out to him that they both provided for their family. They were a team on this.

But one day, Scott had needed some money for a class trip. It hadn't been a great deal, if he remembered correctly, but his mom had gone to the bank and taken it out of the account, her account as it had turned out, because his dad had been stubborn about signing the card to give him access. His dad had been livid. Apparently, he'd thought it was fine for him to go to the bank and ask for a loan rather than to just simply admit that the money would have been all right, no matter the account it came from. So his mom had gone to the bank that afternoon, withdrawn as much as she could, and put it in the fireplace. When Dad had come home that night, she started a fire with some of it and told him if it wasn't their money, there was no point in keeping it. As far as Trent remembered, it was never brought up again, and the money had been put in the family account. Now he'd done the same thing with his own mate.

"What I mean is, we don't need to spend it on this place. I'm pretty sure that they'll cut us a good deal. And if not, then I'll let you buy it for me." She turned in his arms and looked up at him. "I don't want to ever fight with you about money. It's ours. Right?"

"Yes. It's ours. Thank you." She turned back to the water, and he felt her laughter. "You can make it up to me by cleaning the fish for our dinner."

He felt his heart sink. Trent would rather have fought about the money. He knew less about cleaning fish than he did about catching them. They might have to order a pizza if he was in charge of it.

CHAPTER 5

Tanner looked over the paperwork in front of him. It was a timeline of events that led straight to the man who was still trying to get in touch with Trent. He looked at Noah when the chair that he was sitting in creaked. He'd not said a single word since he'd come by Tanner's office earlier this evening, asking to speak to him, and handed over a thick file with the names Cartwright/Ford on it.

"Do you have any questions? You do look like you might have a couple hundred." Tanner nodded, then shook his head. Noah laughed. "I have kept track of the man over the years, knowing that someday he'd raise his head just enough for me to cut it off. Snakes...that's the only way that you can kill them properly, you know. You should also know that Joe kept these notes for me, and she also has a law degree. Several others, as a matter of fact, but she might be able to help you when you need someone. She's that good."

"She's been around." Tanner flushed when he realized what he'd said. "What I meant was she's old. Christ, that's not right either. What I mean is...I have no idea what I mean."

"Yes. Joe has been living a long time. I'm assuming that was what you were trying to say." Tanner told him it was. "As I was saying, Joe has been keeping the notes that you see here. Most of them are done by hand, but I do believe she might have transcribed them for easier reading. You should ask her. When she watches over me during the day, there is little for her to do, so she has become an expert at a great many things."

"What happens with her now?" Noah asked him what he meant. "I mean, she's Trent's mate. I don't know what her plans are now, but I'm sure she's going to want to spend more time with him. Do you need a watcher?"

"Are you volunteering for the job? And it's 'day walker,' not 'watcher.'" Tanner told him he was, actually. "I don't think you'd be cut out for it. I don't doubt that you'd keep me safe, but for the most part Joe was only my day walker because I wanted her to be safe. Had I not taken her in, she would never have survived the times she was born to. Times then were…let's just say that I kept her as safe as she did me. More so if you want to know the truth. But as my day walker, you'd have to lead a very solitary life. Wolves aren't cut out to be alone, from my experience. I think that is why Joe was so good at it. She cared as little for humans as I did at the time."

"She is part of a pack now. I mean, as you said, we're not ones to be alone. She won't…will she continue to work for you?" Noah told him that it was up to her, but her watching over him wasn't as necessary as it had been before computers. "I would imagine that they've done a lot for your kind. Alarms alone would have come a long way from when you were born."

"They have. As have a great many things." Noah glanced at the file before leaning back on the seat he was in.

"Did you know that in a blink of an eye, things could change that would make your hair turn white? Say, the invention of cars for example. One night I was walking along a dark road and this monstrous sound came from behind me. Turning, I saw these two eyes, great shining things that had my heart pounding and me thinking the gates of hell had opened up, and I was surely going to die for my terrible crimes against humans. As I leapt into the grasses along the road, this monster that was nothing more than a car with lights in the front of it drove by me. I lay there for several minutes, trying to wrap my mind around what had just happened. It didn't occur to me until I was home that I could have simply left the area before it got me…I was that terrified."

They both laughed. Tanner could actually see Noah being afraid of such a thing. His grandda, a man who was older than dirt when Tanner was born, had told them over and over about how things had changed too fast for him and his grandmother, and they'd moved to the mountains long ago to be alone. He decided to call them for a visit soon.

Tanner knew that he was avoiding the work in front of him. He needed to process, and he couldn't do that sitting with the paperwork in front of him. He had had to leave the firm he was at recently because it had been too much for him to sit behind his desk all day and not be allowed to roam the halls like he wanted. They apparently frowned upon that and had stifled his mind when they'd confined him to one place for too long. It was leave the well-paying job or go insane. Well, insaner.

"You think that she and Trent will make a good pair?" He knew that wolves mated for life. But there were some things that the two of them would have to overcome that normal wolves didn't even encounter. "She's an immortal, she told us. What happens to her should you get hurt or decide that you want to wash the stench of humans forever off your life?"

"You do have a way with words, don't you, young Tanner? I do believe I like that about you. You are...refreshing and fresh. I think I'd like to hire you. But are you asking me if when I die she will join me? No. She's her own person and can do what she wishes. If you are asking me if, should I perish, would she as well because of the bond we have, that answer is also no. I have made her what she is so that if anything should happen to me, she could go on with her life as she had before. But a good deal better off." Tanner nodded and glanced at the paperwork, then away again. "Trent is an immortal too if they have exchanged blood. Which I'm sure they have, knowing the nature of the wolf. He will not age and grow old and die, leaving her behind."

"Does she know?" Noah told him she did about herself, but not about Trent, at least he didn't think so. "And are you planning to tell them? Because I'm pretty sure that...."

He looked at the paperwork again, sitting down now that what he'd been searching for hit him. He started moving the timeline around. There were two of them here...one was for Ford, the other for his partner, Jefferson Marshall. Tanner started talking as he made the things line up.

"Jefferson only came on the scene about three years ago. An otherwise unknown in the business world, he seemed to have his shit together and enough funds to buy his way into about anything. When he met Ford, he had just been widowed, or so he said in the interview he gave right after joining Ford." He nearly had it the way he wanted, but there was something he was missing. As he continued, he looked through the file regarding Ford. "Ford is a thief. Not only that, he had his hands in a great many pots that seemed to just belly up about the time he was leaving; or in some instances, he'd already left the company. But since Marshall joined him, he's been pretty stable. Not really a standup guy, but someone that seemed to know his business. It wasn't until Elijah and I started working on this project that he and Trent were going to do that we discovered that on the surface he was a good guy, but in the background, he'd not changed one bit."

"You think they're connected somehow, in the past?" Tanner didn't answer Noah. He was missing the thing that connected the dots. As soon as he found it, he laid the picture down on the timeline about four years before Ford had met Marshall. "Sydney?"

"She was the key. Sydney Carlin is somehow going to figure in with this deal they have going. And I'm pretty sure that Ford hasn't seen it yet. Because if he has, he's not really thinking that Jefferson is any sort of threat. Do you know what happened to her after you left her? I mean, that day or a few days thereafter?" Noah picked up the picture of the woman he'd known about ten years ago. "According to this file, she died not long after you were there, within about three weeks. But the article about her doesn't say how. And as far as I can see, there is no obit either. It was as if no one cared enough to even run that. I thought she had a great deal of money?"

"There was never any money. But she was a lovely thing. We had nice walks. Sydney knew what I was, I think, but she never mentioned it and neither did I. We were just friends. She knew Joe as well. Perhaps she would know. We left the area right after Ford was run out of town...might have even been the same day. We were headed out anyway, so I can't remember that timeline very well." Tanner watched the man in front of him and knew he was trying to remember something big. "You might want to try and find a boy...well, he'd be a man by now, but his name was Gibson. I'm not sure of his first name other than I think it started with a B. Brad or Ben. Something like that. He lived in the brownstone next to hers. Younger than her by a few years, but he was infatuated with her. Gave me some trouble once or twice so I had to have a little talk with him. Joe also talked with him, a number of times as a matter of fact. I think they became friends of a sort. Joe could be helpful in answering any questions about him."

"You talked with him how? Did you force him to not see her any longer?" Noah said no, it was just that he explained he had been worried about a single woman living alone and had befriended her, and that was it. "And you don't think he might have hurt her?"

"No. Like I said, he was sort of in love with her. He was a good boy. I don't remember a great deal about him other than he was a slightly overweight, nerdy type that had a great deal of computer knowledge even back then." Tanner made a mental note to see what he could find out. "He did talk about Ford. Only he wasn't Ford then. He was Cartwright. Benson Cartwright. Hated the man on sight, as he had me at first. He might have seen Ford coming and going from Sydney's place and thought the man might hurt her, as he had thought I would. Gibson might be one to talk to as well about what happened to Sydney, other than the fact that she died. I, like you, think there's a connection."

"When you told me about the night that Sydney left Ford, you said that you told her to go home and call her friends. Did she do that? And how exactly did you do it?"

This time Noah got up to pace. Tanner had an idea what he'd done to her, but he wanted to be sure. "Would she have felt guilty about what she'd done to Ford?"

"I did force her to do those things, as you've guessed. It wasn't hard, however. She didn't really trust him as much as Ford thought. In fact, I don't think she liked him at all and found him to be a nuisance. He thought her to be stupid, and that was the sort of woman he preyed on. Still does, as far as I can see. But would she have felt guilty? I don't think so. She was level-headed, smart, and had a good eye for art and saving her money, what little she had of it. I think Ford thought her to be rich. And she did carry herself that way, but she had nothing more than her rent and food money most of the time." He stopped pacing and looked at him. "I keep coming back to the young man that lived next door to her. There was something there, but I never looked into it. Something about him that keeps tugging at my memory."

Tanner got up to get his laptop. He had a desktop computer he used mostly, but he wanted to continue this with all the files in front of him. Putting in the name Gibson and the year with the street name, he hit on it almost immediately.

"He found her body. I mean, that's what the paper says here. His first name was Benny, not a nickname but his birth name. At the time of her death the paper says he was seventeen. And Miss Carlin was only twenty-four." Tanner did a quick image search on his name. "Fuck me. It's him. It's Jefferson Marshall."

He showed the picture to Noah, who sat down hard on the couch. "That's it. That's the tug. I remember the boy turned man. I mean, I can see it as clear as day now. Benny, yes that's it. He really hated Ford then. Fuck. Do you think

Ford knows? Of course not. If he did, he'd call him out or kill him. Death would be what I'd do. But why now? I mean, it's been about ten years. Why do you suppose he's taken so long to do whatever it is he has planned?"

"You said yourself that Ford changed himself. Why, we don't know for sure. It could have been because of you. We both know that he's been hunting you down by way of Joe. He didn't know until last night that you had figured it out. So why is Jefferson after him? Because you know as well as I do that there is no way they just happened to hook up." Tanner looked at the picture and thought the man to be a little nerdy. Much like he supposed he'd been as a child, but more so now. "He's after Ford. For something. And I'd bet it has to do with Miss Carlin."

"No. They did not just happen to hook up. You're right, I'd bet anything on it that he's after Max for something. But what?" He got up to pace again. "We need Joe here. She has a better mind than most people I know. When are they set to return?"

"Well, that could be a problem." Noah asked him why. "Mom told me this morning that Trent has asked to buy the cabin off them. He and Joe want to live there for the rest of their days away from the city."

"Well fuck a duck and watch it waddle." Yeah, Tanner thought, that about summed it up. "I guess we will have to go to them then. When can you be ready to leave?"

They made plans to meet up tomorrow night and then Noah left. He also left behind his paperwork. Tanner knew that he should go to bed, but he had to find a job. Not even his parents knew yet that he'd left his paying job, and he was quickly running out of excuses and money to support himself. Pulling out the paper, he started going through the help wanted pages looking for just about anything right now. But without much in the way of experience as a trucker or a layperson, he wasn't really qualified to do much of anything but be an attorney.

Tanner loved what he did. It was exciting, never the same, and he had made a great deal of money at it. Not that money was everything, but it certainly helped with paying bills and eating. He knew that he could go to his parents and they'd help him out, but he really wanted, and needed, to do this on his own. So marking through the help wanted ads, he decided that tomorrow he'd start looking into fast food. He'd done it before and it had paid pretty well. Being unemployed sucked.

~~~

Trent came into the house with his arms loaded with wood and watched Joe as she cooked. They had worked out an arrangement over the last two days they'd been here together, and it was working out well. She did the cooking and kitchen clean-up, and he did all the rest. He wasn't ashamed to admit that he was doing pretty well as a domestic. The pay was certainly nice. Going into the kitchen where she was, he moved up behind her and nipped at her neck.

"You keep that up and we'll not have any dinner until midnight again. Last night you wore me out." He held her hips while he rocked into her ass. He seemed to be at a constant state of arousal since he'd met her. Not that he was complaining, but he was worried about wearing her out. "Trent, back off if you want to eat tonight."

"I do want to eat tonight." He turned her around and lifted her up to sit her on the nearby counter. Going to the stove again, he turned off all the burners and the oven and moved back to her. "You, as a matter of fact."

"You do know that was our dinner, right?" He nodded and pulled a chair from the table. "What are you thinking you're going to do with that?"

"Well, since I know for a fact that you're wet, I'm going to sit right here and have myself a little appetizer before I have the main course. Then when you've filled me with your creamy goodness, I'm going to strip my pants off and fuck you where you sit. Hard and fast until you scream yourself hoarse." She leaned back on the counter, and he reached up to her hips and pulled her pants and panties off. "Spread your legs for me, baby. Let me have my fun."

When she opened her legs for him, Trent slid his fingers into her. She really was wet, and when her juices started to run down his arm, he leaned in and suckled her clit into his mouth and bit down gently. Her hips started moving up and down off the counter then, and he knew she was close.

Fucking her with his fingers, Trent ate her, lapping at her pussy with his mouth and tongue until he was sure she'd come a half dozen times. Standing up, he opened the fly to his pants and freed his cock. He had to be careful now because he was so hard and full, and he didn't want to catch himself in his zipper. Sliding his crown into her heat, he watched her face.

"You love this don't you? Me playing with you until you come? Will you, baby? Come with me like this?" Her moan nearly made him slam forward, but instead he slid his crown into her sheath and fucked her in short, quick jabs. "I could come like this. Fucking you just enough to make you scream. You have no idea how much I love to have you tighten around me, make me feel like you're milking me with your sheath. Christ, I love you."

She slid her fingers to his cock and every time he slid out of her, she ran her finger around him. He was close now — his balls were full and he wanted to empty himself deep inside of her. Before he could do just that, she grabbed him in her fist and held him.

"Fuck me from behind. I want to feel you slamming your cock into me from behind." He nearly fell back when she gave him a little push. When she got off the counter and turned around, he ran his hand down her ass to her gate, sliding his fingers into her heat. "Fuck me, Trent. I need it hard."

Moving his finger, he grabbed her hips. When she moved her hips back, spreading her legs wider, he fisted his cock and held it at her entrance. The next time she moved back to take him, Trent slammed forward, taking her all the way to the counter as he did so. He knew for as long as he lived he'd never get enough of loving her. Physically or emotionally.

She was crying out now. Each time he pounded her, holding her tightly as he did so, she moved back. And when she screamed she was coming, her body bowing up off the counter and to him, he held her to him as he emptied himself. His body holding hers tightly between the counter and him, Trent bit down hard on her shoulder and heard bones break.

He came again when she lifted his wrist to her mouth and bit him. Trent saw stars then, his vision sliding from perfect to slightly blurry, with brilliant bright bursts of light making his body feel amazing, and he held her as she drank from him. He lifted his head from her shoulder, his cock still semi-hard inside of her, and fucked her slowly while she sealed the wounds she'd created.

When she went limp in his arms, he moved to pick her up and then carried her to the table and the other chair there. Holding her, he wondered how he'd ever be without her, or how he had survived all this time without her in his life. Trent held her to him, stroking her back while they both recovered.

"Dinner is ruined." He laughed and so did she. "I guess we'll have to have cereal now. I don't think I can save the cake either. I was going to surprise you with it. Sort of like a special treat for making me come so many times last night and today."

"Having you in my arms is treat enough. However, if you wanted to bake me up a batch of those biscuits, I'd surely love that. But only one batch. I have to eat better." She didn't move out of his arms, and he was content with that. They were happy. Hell, he was ecstatic. Trent was in love, and feeling better every day.

Last night they'd had the fish he'd caught and the ones she'd caught as well. Trent didn't know for sure, but he thought that there had never been a better cooked meal in the world. They'd had small boiled potatoes as well as green beans with it, and he'd considered himself the king of his castle. Had he had the strength after making love to her twice after they'd eaten, Trent might have gone out on the deck and declared himself king of the beasts. He would have pounded on his chest too. But he had been just too tired to do anything but doze in the chair that looked out over the deck.

When Joe got up and worked on dinner, he pulled his pants up but didn't bother snapping the top button. He was alone but for her and didn't care at the moment. Joe told him that dinner wasn't ruined and she'd have it done in about twenty minutes. He told her what he'd talked about with his brother.

"Tanner was coming up tomorrow night with Noah. They have some information and Tanner needs for you to help him out with it." She said she would. Trent knew that she had a few degrees under her belt, as well as knowing a few other languages. He had been so impressed that he'd had her talk dirty to him in French all night until he just couldn't take it anymore and pounced on her. "Mom and Dad said we could have this house as a wedding gift."

The spatula in her hand dropped. When she turned to him, he reached into his pocket and pulled out the box that his mom had told him was at the cabin. She'd planted it for him so that, in the event things worked out, he'd have it.

"I fell in love with you. I don't know when. It could have been when you walked into the bedroom or when you kissed me the first time." He got down on his knees and moved slowly to her. "I really have no idea, but I do love you. With all that I am."

"You don't have to marry me." He told her that he most certainly did. "Really, I'm content just to be with you. We don't need anything to say that it's okay for us to be together."

"I do." He took her hand in his and kissed her palm before he turned it over again. "I have a ring. My mom, in her amazing wisdom, made sure that I could have something here to ask you with. I am going to have to get her something really nice when I see her the next time."

The ring, he knew, was his grandmother's. It had been in his family for a few generations, and he was glad that she'd thought of it for him. The band alone was a work of art...wolves chasing each other around the gold. The small diamonds that were a part of each collar around them had been set deep in the gold. But the large diamond on the top was what drew attention to it.

The four wolves were on their hind legs and holding the large stone above their chests. Each of them, using their paws beneath it, had their chins on the top to hold it in place. His great-great grandfather had been a jeweler before he'd met his mate, and had fashioned the one of a kind ring for her. Trent put it on Joe's finger, and wasn't surprised that it was a perfect fit.

"Oh Trent, it's beautiful. Are you sure you want me to have it?"

He kissed her hand again and turned the ring so that the wolves were up. "Johanna Samuels, will you do me the honor of marrying me? Love me for the rest of my life? Hold me when I'm whiney? Show me how to relax, fish, and have fun? Will you have children with me, love them with me, and keep them safe?" He stood up then. "I love you with all that I am and ever hope to be. I will cherish each moment with you and keep it in my heart for all time, long after I'm gone. Will you please marry me?"

"I will." Trent kissed her then, feeling her emotion like his own. When he lifted his head to look down at her, she smiled at him and then kissed him quickly on his mouth as she continued. "I love you too. I never thought I'd feel this way, but I do love you. Short time or not, you are my heart and soul, and I will never leave you."

He touched her whenever he could while she finished their dinner. There was more to tell her. A lot more, but not right now. They were happy, and he wanted that to last as long as it could. When she sat a plate in front of him, biscuits and gravy with hash browns and six eggs, he looked at her.

"You've been burning a lot of energy lately. And I for one would like for you to burn a little more." She poured him some juice and sat down with her own plate. "Now, tell me what you don't think I need to hear. I can see on your face that you're keeping something from me."

"We have to go home the day after tomorrow. One of my brothers or my dad is coming to get us. Noah is going to wait to talk to us then, when we get there, about whatever is going on with Ford." She nodded and asked him what else was going on. "I have to work, much as I hate to admit it, and there is this matter with Ford, like I said. He has to be dealt with. Once and for all."

"I agree. He's been a problem for Noah and me for many years. Not a constant one, but enough that we've been keeping an eye on him with each of his movements. He is not a good person, Max Ford." He ate for a few moments before she spoke again. "Tell me when you know something, please. I don't want to have to worry that you're keeping me in the dark. I can't live with that, okay? Not to mention, it makes you stressed out when you think you need to protect me. I'm good with it. All right?"

"Yes. Okay." He nodded, then continued as he ate. "I've been thinking about my life before…well, before you. I'm not going to keep the business I have now. I want to sell to Elijah, if he'll have it, and try something else. I'm not sure yet, but there are…I want to be a teacher. History, and then maybe see if I can coach football too. I played when I was a kid all the way up through college. I want to teach."

"Then you should." He felt better already and asked her what she was going to do. "I have a job. I work for Noah. I know that he really doesn't need for me to be his day walker anymore. There are enough people that can do that now. But I do other things for him…mostly run his businesses, as well as run a few of his other properties. I have many as well, things that I have invested in and properties of my own. They belong to us both now. But I want to do that."

"Then you should." She grinned at him, and he leaned back in his chair to look at her. "Christ, I love you. Where have you been all my life?"

"Wondering when someone was going to come along and try to kill my master. Learning to be a poet, architect, a cook, and a few other things that I enjoy. I took some pottery classes once and painted. I had to fill my time wisely until you came for me." Trent laughed, and so did she. "I love you as well, Trent. And we are going to have so much fun."

He hoped so. But he had to deal with Ford first, and anything that might come along with that. He also had to figure out how to tell his family that he wasn't going to work at his job anymore, and that he wanted to be a teacher. Life, he figured, was about to get very hectic, and he was excited for the ride.

CHAPTER 6

Joe looked at the two pictures of Benny, the young man, and of Jefferson, the adult. It was the same person. But why would he come after Max, if that was what he was going to do? There had to be more than just the fact that he'd been cruel to him as a younger man. The others were talking around her, but she could easily tune them out. It wasn't until TJ, as he had insisted that she call him, sat down next to her that she snapped out of it.

"You see something there?" Joe told him she wasn't sure just yet. "Yeah, I have that feeling sometimes. It's like you're looking too hard at it. Take a break. Talk to me about this thing with my son."

"Thing? I'm not sure I understand what it is you mean." He explained. "You wish to know about him selling his business to Elijah. I would guess that would be a better conversation to have with him, don't you think?"

"I talked to him, but I don't care for his answer. I think there's more. Like for instance, why now?" She said she didn't know. "I think you do. I'm not blaming you. I never thought he was cut out for office work anyway. But teaching? I just never saw that coming."

"He is very smart, your son." TJ agreed with her. "Perhaps he wishes only to teach so that he can be a football coach. He did mention that part several times. Can he only be a coach if he is not a teacher?"

"Good question. I have no idea. But I don't think Trent is any better suited to being a teacher than...it's the being inside part that I think might be hard on him. It's what he complained about when he was working all the time. And he needs a job that has no stress. Being a teacher might get him only part of what he wants, but I don't think it will give him what he needs." Joe wasn't sure it was the stress that bothered Trent or the need to be perfect. At any job he did. "He needs one of them jobs that keeps him out of doors, I think. Like a landscape job."

"Landscaping? I did that for a while. It is quite satisfying to see things that you plant grow. Noah and I own a landscaping business together, and have for many years. It is successful where it is. But it will be up to Trent to decide what he does. I want him happy." TJ assured her that he did as well. "You love your children very much...it shows in everything you do. Trent respects you as well. That is a part of everything that he does."

"They're my life," TJ said without any hesitation and with a great deal of conviction. "Christine and I, we would die for our children, much like I'm sure your parents would have done for you."

"My mother was a house servant for a very wealthy man. When he found out that my mother carried me, his bastard, he took her into his home and kept her well fed and happy. But when I was born a female, he fired her, had her return all the good things he'd given her as she lay resting from my birth. I was put out when I was old enough to care for myself. There were times when it was difficult to survive during those times. But I was resourceful and kept myself alive. Then I met Noah, and he gave me a part of him so that I could live a long and very good life." TJ told her he was sorry. "Don't be. It's not your fault. It was just the way things were then. Now people do worse things to children they no longer wish to keep. I have seen dogs treated with better manners. Haven't you?"

"Yes. Sadly." TJ leaned back on the couch they were sharing. He was a very nice man, and he and his wife had been very happy that she and Trent were getting married soon. "Do you think it's possible that Ford killed this woman and Marshall saw him do it?"

"I thought the same, but there is no way of finding out after all this time. The newspaper said that her death was suspicious, but I cannot find where there was any solving of it. If it was indeed murder, no one seemed to care enough to go and find the person or persons who had done it, and the case, even after all these years, is unsolved. So I think the lack of interest had them shoving it under the rug for a time until it was simply out of their memories completely. She had no family to mourn her, and she had nothing to leave anyone should they have cared. I think she was cremated as a way for the city not to have to bury her."

"But this boy, he found her, correct? Do you think he might have killed her? Over something he had in his head, like that she belonged to him?" Joe said that she didn't think that either. "He was in love with her, Noah said. You thinking there might have been something there? Not murder, but something that happened that he saw?"

"I don't know. I suppose that could be it. As you said, he was, for all intents and purposes, in love with her. I spoke to him several times before she was killed. He was simply a nice boy who thought that he could give her a better life." Joe wondered now if he might have given her more than Max would have. "He told me once that Max had tried to hurt her on several occasions when she wouldn't allow him into her home. I think perhaps that might have upset him, but he always just said that she'd handled herself well but that he'd be there if she needed him. I'm not sure what he meant by Max hurting her. Even now, I don't know."

"So this young man tried to keep Ford away from a woman that he wanted to rob. There were issues with her and Ford...everyone that knew them could attest to that. Then Ford was ridiculed, left town, and she ended up dead a few weeks later." She told him that was what it looked like. "But something drove this kid, now a man, to more than likely seek out Ford and make him...what? Pay for some crime that only Jefferson knew about?"

"That is what it seems like. But it is my understanding that Noah and Randal are going to talk to him. Tomorrow, correct?" TJ said that was right but that he wasn't happy about that. "Noah won't let anything happen to your son. You have my word on that."

"I know that. I mean in the short time I've known the man, I think he's a good guy. What I worry about is if Jefferson is no more upstanding than Ford is. What if they're in this together to get back at Noah?" Joe had thought of that as well. "I'd like nothing better than to meet him myself. See his worth."

"Then you should go as well." He looked at her oddly. "You are the patriarch of this family; should they not listen to you when you ask for something?"

"Yeah, you'd think that, wouldn't you?" Joe didn't understand what he meant, but before she could ask him to explain, he snapped his fingers as if just remembering something. "The alpha, he wants to see the two of you. Soon. I don't think he'll have a problem with the two of you becoming mates, but there are things he has to make sure you know. I'm sure that will be nothing more than you going to pledge yourself to him and what not. He was…he did seem sort of put out to know that Trent had found his mate, but I don't know why. You'd think he'd be happy about it, wouldn't you?"

"Perhaps he thinks that Trent will want more now that he has his own family. I don't know this alpha, nor have I heard anything about him other than his name is Casey O'Neal." She knew that the Calhoun family followed the laws and ways of their pack. It had surprised her and Noah that TJ had not become the leader of their group when he'd turned twenty-five. He was strong enough and he was respected a great deal, as were all the Calhouns. She told him that she'd talk to Trent and see what he wanted to do concerning the other male.

When she was left alone, she looked at the police report again. She had seen many such reports given by the police when she'd been an attorney, but this one seemed to be lacking in a great many areas.

In the area where it said official cause of death, there were four things to choose from, yet none were marked. But the picture of wounds on the drawing of the deceased bothered her most of all.

The drawing was a copy of a non-descript female. The same kind of drawing was available for a male should they have needed it. The coroner in this case had marked several places that Sydney had injuries, but had offered no explanation of how they might have gotten there. For example, there was a deep puncture wound on her left thigh. All it had was the words deep and puncture. Then there were the ligature marks on her wrists. There, too, it only pointed them out without explaining anything about them. Were they from cuffs, someone holding her, or was there tape residue there? No information at all. On the right side of her head was a cut, like she'd fallen or been hit. It looked, according to the picture, like it had run the entire length of her forehead, yet there was nothing about whether or not it had been made by a knife or a fall. The scrapes on her knuckles might had been from her defending herself. And her mouth had been cut as well. Some notes on the body could have been done better as well, to Joe's way of thinking.

"Was she raped?" Joe looked at Sterling when he asked. Joe told him she thought so, but the report hadn't mentioned a rape kit being used. "I've looked over the entire file, and there is no report of any kind of tests being made on her...no toxicology or any kind of skin or tissue searches. To me, and I'm not much of a sleuth, she looks like someone either raped her or tried. Was she naked when found?"

"No. Her clothing was intact." She looked at Sterling again before continuing. "I think perhaps Jefferson cleaned her up after he found her and called the police. I don't know why I think that, but I can see him doing such a thing. He wouldn't want her to be exposed like that. He would have wanted her to have dignity even in death."

"I can see that too." He picked up the paper she had been studying and then put it back down. "I have a friend that can go over these for us. I don't know when he can look, but I can ask him. As lay-persons, we might just be looking at a formal report on someone that we don't know well. At least I didn't know her well."

"That would be very nice." She picked up the papers to put into the file when a small sheet fell out. Leaning over to pick it up, she nearly dropped it again when she realized what it was. "Did you see this?"

She handed to him, and he looked at her after reading it. Sterling looked as shocked as she was. "It says she was pregnant, and that it had been aborted at her death. That she...you think it was Ford's?"

"I don't know what to think. But I should like to speak to Jefferson. I think he needs to explain things to us now. Something about this says that all of this is revenge and this is the key." Sterling nodded to her and stood up. When she did as well, they made their way to Trent. This was going to be the end of it all, she knew it.

~~~

Jefferson didn't bother picking up the file he'd been given...he knew what was in it. Knew every word of every sheet that was there. He even had copies of things that this person didn't. Nothing they could say to him could get him to admit to or corroborate their thinking.

"You know her?" He said nothing to Trent Calhoun. "Jefferson, we want to help you with this. If Ford did you wrong, we can help you."

"I don't understand why you believe, first of all, that I need your help or that I have anything to do with these people. Ford is my partner. A very shady one I've come to find out, but my partner all the same." Jefferson didn't look over at the pictures that hung on his walls and were framed on the shelves that cluttered his office. Why he'd agreed to this meeting he was still trying to figure out, but they were here and he'd do what it took to get them off his back. It was too soon for him to be exposed just yet.

He knew these men, or at least he knew one of them...the others he knew only in that he'd looked into their lives. Noah, the only one that he'd met before, had not said a word to anyone upon entering his home. It made him nervous, him being in his home or anywhere near him for that matter. He wasn't afraid of Noah; he had been at one time, but now he was just fearful that he knew things that Jefferson wished that he didn't. Jefferson was terrified that he knew who he was.

"We believe that you might hold a grudge against Max and are in partnership with him for a reason other than for it to be beneficial to both of you." Well, no shit, he wanted to tell TJ, but said nothing. "We also think that you're this young man Benny Gibson, a young lad that might know something about Ford that the police haven't figured out. About the death of Sydney Carlin."

It hurt him to hear her name, ripped at his heart in ways these men would never, could never understand. He had loved her with all that he'd been. She might have been older than him, even smarter, but she had been his one and only true love. And until he was satisfied that justice was served in her death, he would do whatever it took to make sure her killer saw the errors of his ways. Even if it was served by him and only him.

Even after all these years, he hurt for her. She was by far the nicest person he'd ever known, and she had not deserved what had happened to her. But telling these men what he knew would do none of them any good. The only person who was going to pay was Ford. And he was going to pay dearly.

"Benny? That's your name, isn't it?" He looked at Noah, a man who had not aged one single bit in all these years. It had frightened him a little, seeing the man at his doorstep. And he'd nearly said no when asked if he could be invited in. When he asked him again about being Benny, Jefferson shook his head just as Noah continued. "I'm a vampire. You might not have known that back then, but I'm telling you now. The reason for this full disclosure is that a vampire never forgets a scent. And I have yours. You are without a doubt Benny Gibson."

"There are no such things as vampires." Jefferson tried not to squirm on his seat, and stared right at Noah. "I don't know what you think you're doing, but I'm not stupid. And I think it's time that you—"

"I'm a wolf. Not the horror story sort that you see on television, but I'm one all the same." Trent stood up then and walked toward him. "I'm going to show you something. Just please, don't scream. We don't want to bring the house down on us." He started to tell the man that he had no intentions of screaming when Trent pulled up his sleeve. In a matter of seconds, his hand disappeared and was replaced with a thick wolf paw. The hair on his arm grew and became denser as well. Jefferson whimpered a little when he put the large paw on his own hand. "I'm as real as you are, and as real as the fact that Noah is a vampire."

Jefferson sat very still. He wasn't sure what to believe, but Trent moved back from him and he let out a long breath. These people had to go. But before he could stand up to show them out, TJ spoke again.

"She was with child, did you know that?" Jefferson felt his entire body sag. "They didn't make it known. No one did a test to see if she was raped or not, but now that I'm thinking on it, I can see why they'd not do that. She lost it. There had to be a rape, didn't there, Benny? That wouldn't be how she got pregnant of course, but they did very little to find out who killed her or even why. If that had been one of mine, child or friend, I would have wanted to exact revenge on them. Hard and fast. But you waited…why is that?"

"Benny died that day. I knew she was…the baby wasn't mine, if that's what you're thinking. But the police…they told me if I kept my mouth shut on what I'd seen then they'd not arrest me for tampering with evidence." He reached in his bottom desk drawer and handed TJ the file he'd kept all these years, adding to it when he found things, taking out information that wasn't right. "The officer on duty, he accused me of killing her. Had me in cuffs as they walked around her little living room, messing with her things. Said that it was why I'd redressed her and made sure that she wasn't like that when they got there. I did do that. I…she was so exposed, and I knew that she'd hate that more than anything. But I didn't kill her, and after a while, they left me alone."

"How did they know for sure you didn't kill her? I don't think you did either, but there had to be a reason for them to have let you off for it."

He nodded at TJ, then looked at Trent. "A man told me he could not smell me on her, not sexually. I had no idea what he meant until years later, when I figured out that Joe wasn't human either. She…she was my friend as well." Noah told him that she was marrying Trent. "I liked her a great deal, still do. And you. You never treated me as a child. And when I told you that day that I loved her, you didn't say I was too young or that it wasn't love. You were…nice to me. Not like Max was. Still is for that matter. You treated me like a person, not a kid still in diapers."

"You loved her, of that I have no doubt." Jefferson nodded at TJ and then pulled out another file, this one filled with pictures.

"When the police took away her body — wrapped her up like she was nothing more than the afternoon trash — I snuck back in the room and took what I could. There wasn't much. She didn't have much in the way of personal things. A few pictures and some small cheap jewelry. The place that she lived belonged to my father and she paid him rent." He handed him the first of many pictures that he'd taken from the apartment that day. "That was of us. We'd been out for the day...I was showing her the sights. We weren't...we were friends, not lovers. The child she carried belonged to someone I think she knew briefly."

"Did you see who killed her?" He nodded at Noah, knowing for some reason that this man would understand his anger more than others. "Was it Ford? Is he not just responsible for her death but her losing her child as well?"

"He'd gone back to her place several days after the ad had come out in the paper. My father was furious about it, that one of his tenants had been bothered by such a man. My parents liked Sydney and sort of knew that I was...we were friends, and my parents didn't have a problem with us being together. I could talk to her when I couldn't them. When Max, as he goes by now, came around the afternoon that the article came out about him, my father ran him off with a shotgun. It was a sight that I'll never forget." He grinned at the memory. "Then that night while the household slept and my parents were out with some friends, I went to see her. We often talked well into the night. She would tell me about talks that she had with you, and I would tell her of my plans to be a rich and famous person. One that could take her away from all that. She told me of her child that night."

He remembered the conversation as if he were there again. "I'm going to have a baby. It's not with a person that I love, but a mistake that I made. I want to keep it, but I'm afraid that I just can't raise a baby. I can barely raise the rent." She'd meant it as a joke, but he didn't laugh. "If only you were a little older, Benny. I'd let you care for me."

"I will." She shook her head and told him it was too late for them. "No, it can't be. I'm in love with you, and will be forever."

Her face had looked so sad that he had felt his heart twist up. He knew that she was going to tell him he was nothing more than a baby and much too young to care for himself, much as she'd said about herself.

"And I love you as well, but not like a woman would a man she will keep in her heart like that. You are and will forever be my best friend. I will call on you when I'm in need, and you'll come to me then. But this baby? I can't raise it alone. I'm going to have to give it up. I've no way of supporting a child right, and I want the very best for it. I can't do that. Neither can you, and you know it. We are both victims of our circumstances." He'd not understood her then, but he did think about her words often. Looking at the men in front of him again, shaking off the memory of her words, he finished his story.

"It was well after midnight when I went home to get something for her. I had taken to writing down prose, and she would tell me where I'd misspelled something or what needed work. As I was returning, I heard her speaking. I thought she was on the phone, but when I came all the way into her living room, I could see Max there." Jefferson remembered thinking at the time he should have gone and called his dad. Every time he thought of Max and Sydney that night, he knew that he'd been just as responsible for her death as Max had been. Maybe more so.

Jefferson got up to pace. He could no longer sit there and have them…they would think him a coward. He did that often enough. So he paced so that he'd not have to see their faces when he told them the rest of what had happened that night.

"Max told her that it was her fault that he'd been run out of town. He blamed her for his landlord demanding his rent too. Something I guess he'd let go for a few months, I found out later. I also found out a great many things, but…. When she told him that she had done it, taken out the ad in the paper and would again, he slapped her." His steps grew slower as he remembered it all. "As she lay there, bleeding from her head, he tied her arms above her head and then cut her clothing off. When she woke, screaming at him, he took a pillow and stuffed it over her face while he…he—"

"He raped her." Jefferson nodded at Trent. "Go on. What did he do next? There were cuts to her leg and a wound on her head."

"She hit the fireplace when she went down. I think that was what had knocked her out at first. The cut on her leg happened when Max used a knife to cut away her clothing. I saw him cut deeply into her, then laugh about it." He waited for them, any of them, to ask him why he'd not saved her, but they all sat there, waiting on him to finish. "After he raped her, she bled a great deal. I think that might have been when she lost her child. But when he stood up, pulling his clothing back on himself, I could see that she was dead. Her chest no longer moved when he moved the pillow off her face."

"Did he see you?" Jefferson shook his head at Noah's question. "You did the right thing, Jefferson. Had you gone in there with him, tried to help her in any way, you would have died as well. You know that, don't you?"

"I could have saved her." He broke down then, admitting for the first time in his short life that he'd done nothing to help her. He sobbed, like the child he'd been all those years ago when he'd let the only woman he'd ever love lay there and be killed. "She lay there, broken and bleeding, and I did nothing."

"But you did. You saved her dignity and you were her friend. Are you the one that put the marker on her grave?" He nodded, not knowing how Noah would have been able to find that out. "I went to the city records and did some digging. I found that a person who wanted to remain anonymous had requested her ashes, and they were buried soon after. I knew that it had to be you when we starting putting two and two together. That was very kind of you. I wish I could have helped you with that. It was a great undertaking that you've done for her."

"She might be alive had I done something sooner." TJ told him that he'd be dead too, that Max was a ruthless bastard. "You don't know the half of it. He's a slimy bastard too. And more than that, I think that he's killed more than just Sydney. Also, I wanted to say that I'm glad that you pulled from the deal when you did. I didn't know until after the fact what he was up to with your company. I want to ruin him, but not at the expense of others."

"What is he up to, do you know?" Jefferson nodded at Trent and went to his desk again and pulled out a small remote. The projector slid from the wall at the press of a button, and he touched his fingers to the camera behind him. "That's quite impressive, if I do say so myself."

"It was in the house when I bought it. I fell in love with watching old reel to reels that I would find. Sorry, but this is just a thumb drive of a conversation that I got when Max had a meeting in his office. And yes, I bugged his offices and his home, as well as his cars and some of his jewelry. I know everything there is to know about the man." He grinned at Trent when he told him he needed him to come work for him. "My parents were indulgent and got me all the newest gadgets that came along. I miss them dearly, but they left me very comfortable. I will help you with projects...it would be my pleasure to do so. But this conversation, it was taken a few weeks ago."

As the video ran, he sat down and watched them instead of the recording. He knew it by heart, every word, every gesture, as well as the amount of money that was exchanged between the two men. There wasn't anything in there that could be used in a court of law, but plenty enough to make these men aware of the bastard they had nearly done business with.

Max had made a deal with the devil. Not only that, but he'd really fucked everyone over in a very short amount of time while he'd been at it. This man was there to get the money that had been earmarked to pay the retirement funds of the people that worked for them. The money was going to an overseas account, and this man was only one of several who was sending it there for him. Jefferson had put it back and kept Max from it, but it did show how ruthless and terrible a person Max really was. Then he watched Trent carefully when Max talked about the loan he was getting from the man's firm.

"Christ, he was going to take it all and run." Jefferson nodded at Trent. "I would have been bankrupt. I mean...Christ, I would have gone to jail if this hadn't been stopped. He was saying things…the man was going to ruin me. And for what? A few million dollars? What the fuck was I supposed to do? I can't believe this."

"He would have killed you as well. It's the way that he does things." He handed him the last sheet of paper. "And he has a list of men that were to murder you so he could collect on the insurance policy that he'd taken out on you. I've taken the liberty of cancelling the hits and changing the beneficiaries to your parents' names. I do hope that is all right."

Trent nodded as they rewound and watched the video again. The man in the shot was now dead; he'd been killed a few days ago. Jefferson wasn't sure who had done it, but he was reasonably sure it had been Max. The man had wanted his money up front, and Max didn't have it…and never would. Now he was lying in a morgue without a name to go with his body, and Jefferson was sure, like with Sydney, there were many more bodies.

"I'm going to ruin the man. I'm going to make sure that he pays for every crime that I've found on him. And when he's caught, I'm going to tell him just who I am." Noah said he'd like to help. "I think I'd like that."

CHAPTER 7

"I should like to talk to you, Trent." To be honest, Noah was sort of nervous about the big wolf and talking to him about Joe. "There are some things that I think I need to clear up with you."

"I've already told her that her money is fine where it is. It's ours. Both of ours. She made me understand that." Noah wondered how that had gone over, and nearly burst out laughing when the young pup frowned before continuing. "I won't make that mistake again. Our money is just that, our money. She's very touchy about that, isn't she?"

"Yes. That stems, I believe, from not having much. She's worked very hard at getting where she is, and I think that the two of you will do well with her knowledge of business and other things. But that wasn't what I meant to tell you. It's about her powers." Trent asked him just how much Joe was worth. "Quite a bit. Even by my standards, she has a good deal of money. Billions by now, I would guess. As I said, she's been working hard to save her—"

"You mean millions." Noah covered his mouth to hide the smile and shook his head. "You said billions, but I think you meant millions, right? I mean, not that millions isn't a lot, but billions is a fucking lot."

"Yes, I'm well aware of how much billions is. And she has a few of them. Last I had any knowledge of it, I think it was right around seven. Probably more by now." Noah grabbed Trent as his knees simply gave out on him. When he was safely in the chair, Noah sat as well. "She will be most upset with me if you faint away while in my care. And I have a great many things to tell you as yet."

"I thought you were joking with me. I knew she had a lot saved. She told me that you paid her well and that she was good at investing in companies. I mean, you know, millions of dollars is a lot for even the average person to save. She has been around for a while now and would have been able to save a great deal, I guess. And she told me that she watches trends and markets. I'm babbling, I'm sorry. I'm not usually so disjointed when I talk." Noah told him that was what he wanted to talk to him about. "Trends or markets? Because if it's about a loan, I've made a deal with my brother and he's taking over the business. I'm sorry."

"No. It's about being around for a long time. You will be too." Trent nodded. Noah knew he was still thinking about the amount of money that Joe had amassed. "You're like her, in a great many things. Like immortality. And a few other perks. Like you can heal much faster. As a wolf, you could anyway, but now it will be as if you are healing as you—"

"What did you say?" Noah told him. "No. Not the healing part. The immortality part. I'm not an immortal. Joe told me that she was, because of something you did to her. But I'm only a human, and, while I'll live a little longer than a regular person, I'm going to die."

"No, you won't. You're just like Joe. All of her. The moment you accepted her blood into your body as her mate, you became as she is. It's one of the things that I was able to give her as my friend too." Trent was shaking his head. "You didn't expect to die in a few years and leave her, did you? It's the way that things work with our kind. Well, my kind. I'm very powerful. I've been around for a very long time, Trent, longer than Joe by a great many centuries."

"She's a watcher, not a vampire." Noah told him that it was day walker, not watcher. "What's the difference?"

"A day walker affords all the benefits of being a vampire but doesn't have to drink blood, nor does the sun bother her. A watcher is someone that has been risen from the dead, a person who only does what his master commands him to do and will kill anything and everything that comes between him and his master, and is loyal only to him. Ever. Joe has never died. She is not...I think you call them zombies. She is not one of those...she's a day walker. For me."

"And so...I'm sorry, but I'm trying to understand this." Noah told him it was fine. He was actually enjoying watching the man work through his fears. "So what happens to her should you...you die or be killed? Will she die as well?"

"No. She's an immortal. As are you. The only way to kill you—and it's not something that happens anymore—is that you would have to be beheaded 'on consecrated ground by a man of the cloth who has no sins of his own.' The last part is what most people fail on. Even if they are a good clergy, they have some small sin in their past. Very few people could say that they have no sins. When I die, and I would imagine I will one day, I will simply meet the sun and Joe will continue as if nothing happened. I do hope that she will shed a small tear for me, but I don't know."

Noah had hoped for a laugh, or at the very least a small smile. But the poor boy was having trouble wrapping his mind around everything right now. When he got up to go to the window, Noah watched him.

There was a calmness about Trent now that hadn't been there before meeting Joe. Noah knew, from Trent's father, that Trent had been stressed long before the heart attack that had brought the entire family to their knees. And like the rest of the family, Noah was glad for the couple, happy that they were so much in love.

Noah liked Trent. A great deal. Had he been able to pick a mate for his Joe, this would have been the perfect man for her. He was smart, but willing to admit when he was wrong. He had money...not as much as Joe, but he wasn't poor either. A home, a good solid family, and as far as Noah could see, he loved Joe. Very much so.

"Can we have children?" Noah told him that they could have as many as they wished for as long as they wanted. "And will they be like us? Immortal as well?"

"Yes." Noah was almost fearful of the next confession he had. "As are your parents and brothers. I did not think that you'd want to watch them grow old and die any more than I would. I have come to love your family very much."

"And they have you as well. But this is a lot to take in." Noah said he'd come to it sooner rather than later. "We have this thing with Max and Jefferson. I've sold my business and now I have a mate. And I have a meeting with the alpha in a few days, which is going to be all right, I think, but something more that I have to deal with right now. I'm not sure how much more I can take on and still be...well, okay with it all. Just so you know, you're going to tell my family what you've done. And so we're on the same page here, I don't think they're going to take it any better than I did, and that wasn't really all that well."

"I will tell them. Perhaps in an email or on the phone. And all these things will work themselves out." Trent asked him if he really believed that. "Not really, but it did sound pretty good, don't you think?"

"I don't think I like you very—" Every part of his body tensed. Noah stood up too when the man looked at him. "Joe is in trouble."

Trent's shift from man to beast was immediate and profoundly beautiful. As he leapt though the door that led out onto the deck, leaving glass and splinters of wood in his wake, Noah reached for his child and hit a hard wall. Before he could try and punch though the barrier, both TJ and his wife came into the room, their fear as evident as it had been on young Trent's face before he left. Noah told them what Trent had said before he'd left them. When they turned to the now broken door, they all watched as five more wolves headed in the direction that Trent had gone.

"They'll get to her." Noah tried again to reach for Joe as Christine soothed her own frayed nerves by talking softly to them. "Whatever it is, they'll protect her."

~~~

Joe didn't panic. Never. But right now, with all this going on around her, it was all she could do not to give in to it. The bank that she was in, and had been in millions of times over the years, was being robbed. And they were doing so without care for who they killed or hurt.

Two were dead already, and one was hurt so badly that Joe knew that without immediate medical attention, they would also be on the list of the dead. There were many others that were bleeding, some not so badly, others bad enough that she feared for them as well. The robbers had come in, shot several of the patrons, and had ordered them on the floor as the doors were being locked down.

After contacting Trent to tell him why she was going to be delayed, he told her that he was coming to her. She had felt better after hearing that, but now she was worried for his safety as well as those with her. It had been an hour since she'd first called out to him, and now he was telling her that the police were doing all that they could. She had no more faith in them than she did the robbers.

She felt the small touch of Trent against her mind before he asked her if she was all right. *I am. I've tried to figure out how many men are here as you asked me to do. There are four that I've counted, but I know there are more. One of them is using a cell phone to talk to someone, but they aren't here where I am. Do you suppose that there are others out there where you are?*

The police have stumbled onto them. I don't know who they're talking to in there, but it's not the guys out here. One of them is dead and the other isn't talking. Or I should say that he can't. They're taking him to the hospital now. How many customers are there in the bank, do you think? She told him there were nine with her and two of them were dead. *The bank manager one of the living?*

He's alive and sitting across from me. He's been hit but not terribly so. I think he is more worried for his face than what is going on right now. He has asked the man next to him if it will leave a mark several times. Do you suppose that he's in on this?

I've been talking to a few of the officers out here, and they're thinking that he was but has since changed his mind. I don't know why they'd know that, but that's what I've been able to find out. She asked him if they were going to get them out of there before the idiots started shooting again. *You just sit tight, love, we're coming for you.*

For some reason Joe thought that he wasn't working with the police on this rescue. And if he was, it was going to be by his rules and not theirs. When she looked around the room again, she had a thought about the people there with her and wondered if any of them were working with the robbers as well. Reaching into the mind of the manager, she found out a great deal more than she'd bargained for.

The manager is in on it. And he's also the one that called the police. The combination of the vault that the robbers want into has been changed, and he doesn't know who might have done it. He thinks he's only alive because they believe he knows the way in, but is holding out for more money. He asked her how she knew that and she told him. *I reached into his mind. Also, he's been going to the vault several times a day and taking out some cash for himself. He's afraid now that whoever changed the locking code also knows about his theft, and he might go to prison. I think that's a good possibility, don't you?*

Oh yeah, that's a done deal. Honey, in a few minutes we're coming in. There is a wolf on the force that is going to let us walk into the basement that will lead us to you and the people that are on the floor you're on. She told him again that she had no idea who else was in the building. *I don't know either, but there are six of us as wolves, and we're not waiting around for someone else to get hurt.*

When you enter the building, close your eyes and then when you open them, I think I can see what you see. I've never done it before, but Noah said that it was one of the things he'd given me to keep me safe. He told her Noah had said he had the same powers she had, and asked her if she thought he could do it as well. *That's wonderful. Yes, you can do it. Just concentrate on what heartbeats you can hear coming close to you. Then you can reach out to them and see if they are friend or foe by entering their mind. Don't push. If you do, you can hurt them.*

All right. I can do that. He paused for several minutes. *We're in the building. Elijah and I are going to take the floor that you're on, and Sterling and Randal are going up to the third floor. Scott and Tanner are going to stay here to keep anyone from coming in or going out that shouldn't be.*

She told him to be careful. *And when you come to this floor, let me know and I'll see if I can tell you where the men with guns are.*

The woman next to her started sobbing, which she'd been doing off and on for the last hour, and it was starting to make Joe nervous. The noise alone was enough to make her want to smack the woman, but when she started wailing, Joe wanted to tell her to shut up and stop acting like a baby.

Stretching her neck, she saw a movement out of the corner of her eye that wasn't Trent or his brothers. She had no idea how she knew that, but she knew as surely as she was sitting there that it wasn't any of them. The big wolf moved along the desks, sniffing the chairs, then moving on. She'd bet anything that it was seeing how many shifters were there with him. She reached out to let Trent know.

What does he look like? I mean, is there anything about him that sticks out? Like markings or his coloring? Joe tried her best not to stare, but could see that he walked with a limp and had a long scar down his right side. *You're sure? His right side?*

Yes, I'm sure. I guess I could tell you that he's facing me and that's how I'm telling you what side it's on, but it's his right. Do you know him?

When Trent didn't answer her, she watched the wolf closely while trying her best not to look as if she was. Reaching into his mind wasn't going to work, because she had a feeling that he would feel her clumsy touch. She knew then that as soon as this was over, she was going to practice this more until she was as good as Noah was. Then she remembered him. Reaching out to him, she could feel his fear for her.

I've been trying to contact you, child. It's been as if I have been hitting a blank wall. Are you all right? She told him what Trent was doing and about the big wolf. *Look at him and then close your eyes for me. Perhaps I can help this way. I don't know who could be there either, but between the two of us, we should be able to figure it out for the pack.*

When she did as he asked, Joe knew who they were looking at. Before she could tell Trent what she and Noah had discovered, she heard a loud scream. Looking at the wolf and what he was doing, Joe felt her belly lurch up as the animal dragged a man away by his throat.

He's cat...panther, I think. Joe said nothing as the man was killed there in front of her. *Don't look, child. You can do nothing for him now. Just be very still and I'll let Trent know that his alpha is in the building with him and will know that he's close.*

I have to do something. He told her to wait. *I can't wait and you know it. When he smells you or even Trent on me, he's going to be really pissed off. Their alpha his going to kill everyone here because of me.*

You don't know that.

But she did know, and told Noah that the wolf was coming toward her, and was now standing in front of her with blood dripping off his muzzle. He could smell her, was all her mind could think about, and when he tensed up and looked to his right, she knew that Trent had entered the room. He looked back at her then, his teeth bared and the hair on his back standing up. He knew that she'd contacted Trent and the others.

She never took her eyes off the big wolf standing over her. Neither of them, it seemed, was going to be the first to look away. But when he was suddenly gone, his face just seconds from being at her throat, Joe closed her eyes for a second to let the fear of what he might have done to her wash over her. Then she opened them and stood up.

Trent had attacked the alpha, she knew that much. And she knew that he'd not looked around for the men with guns before coming to her. She had a fear that one of the others would shoot him, and Joe had to protect him.

Trent and the wolf, the alpha, were fighting now, their bodies knocking over anything and everything that was close enough to be destroyed. She saw Elijah as he made his way to her just as she broke the neck of the first gunman that she came upon.

"Lead them to the lower levels." He shook his head at her. "I have to go and make sure that no one else is on this floor. If they get hurt over this, no one will come out a winner."

At his indecision, she moved to the offices to her right. A gunman was just coming out of the room to no doubt see about the noise, and Joe grabbed him from behind and snapped his neck too. Elijah nodded once, as if he realized she could care for herself, and started for the group on the floor. None of them moved.

"You want them to kill you too? They will if the gunmen come here and see what's going on. Go with him or you'll die. I've no energy to try and help those that do not care to help themselves." The sobber looked at her, then at the wolf, and whined about him biting her. "I see. So you think that a bite is so much deadlier than a bullet? It's not. And he won't bite you. Get up off your asses and get the hell out of here. Damn it, what is wrong with you people?"

One by one they got up. The manager was still sitting there when Elijah led the group toward the stairs. She looked at him and told him to get going. He shook his head, his face full of anger.

"What have you done?" She asked him what he meant. "They have to rob this place. Do you have any idea what they're going to do to me when they don't get their money? Not to mention what is going to happen to me if they get away. The higher-ups are going to think that I've robbed my own bank. You have to sit down and let this play out or there will be hell to pay."

"I don't think so. You should have thought of that before you made this bank and these people's money your own personal pay thing." He shook his head and she nodded at him. "You've taken so much money that didn't belong to you that you're going to be lucky if you only go to jail. These people will lynch you. Also, the authorities already know that you're in on this. So get your slimy ass out of here and face your problems."

He was still sitting there when she moved into the other part of the floor. Joe had enough problems right now, and not one of them was about the bank manager. The third robber was standing with his gun pointed at the alpha and Trent when she cleared her throat. He tensed but didn't look at her just then.

"You cannot kill him, I'm afraid. It won't work for me, you see." He looked in her direction as he pointed the gun at her. "I don't think that's in your best interest either. I need for you to lower your weapon. I'm not going to hurt you too badly if you only do what I tell you."

The pain of the shot took her breath away. But before she could take the gun from the man, he, like the alpha, was simply gone. Elijah had come back and was tearing the man's throat out before she could move. She dropped to her knees, and Elijah came to her and whimpered quietly.

"I'm fine, I promise. The wound will be healed in a few minutes." She put her forehead to his. "You saved me a great deal of pain. I can't thank you enough. I never knew that it hurt so badly to be shot. Did you?"

When he licked her face, she stood up. Trent was coming toward her, and his wolf looked as fit and sexy as she'd ever seen him. Elijah stood beside her and didn't move when she was knocked to the floor so that her back was on it and Trent was laying over her.

Are you hurt? She told him what had happened. *You ever do that again and I will beat your pretty ass for you. I need you in my life.*

"And I you. But there are others here that need to be taken care of. Several more that have been hurt." He didn't move, but Elijah did. "Trent, are you all right?"

Yes. The pause scared her a little. *He's dead. The alpha is dead. I'm not sure what's going to happen to him, but you can bet that someone is going to be pissed off.*

Joe knew what should happen now. Trent had killed the alpha, and that meant he was king. If no one protested it, Trent would take his place as the pack leader. Not that she didn't think he'd do a wonderful job at it.

There were still things they had to do before the police entered the bank. One of them was to get Trent and his brothers out. She reached out to Noah and told him what she needed. He said he'd do it with pleasure.

"Noah is going to alter the minds of the humans to keep them from telling anyone that several big wolves were here. I don't know what they'll tell the police, but you won't be brought up." He looked down at her as she continued. "We have to get the rest of the people out of here though. I'll lead them out once the other robbers are taken care of."

They're all dead now. The others, my brothers, have taken care of them, as well as the cameras in the halls. She'd never thought of that and was glad that he had. But he still hadn't moved. *Dad is on his way here with clothing for us. I'll go out in...I love you, Joe.*

Then he was gone. She wanted to call him back to tell him that she loved him as well, but there were things that had to be taken care of now. Later, she told herself, she'd make him pay for running off. Smiling, she thought of all the things she wanted to do to him.

As she lay there, her mind going a million miles a minute, she heard the door opening to the front of the bank and sat up. When someone told her to put her hands on her head and not to move, Joe obeyed. There was no point in making someone else mad enough to hurt her.

The bank was secured by the police in a matter of twenty minutes. Then the questioning began.

"Are you telling me that you don't know what happened to anyone?" She told the officer again that she didn't know. "You were right there, in the main part of the building, and you don't know what happened to the gunmen or the naked man in the hall."

"No. I've told you several times already that I didn't see anything, as they had us on the floor. I didn't want to get killed." He looked at the blood on her shirt. It was hers, but she'd told him she'd tried to help one of the other people. "I'm not going to tell you again that I don't know what was going on other than we were told to shut up and to sit still."

"You do know that there are six dead men in the building, not counting the naked one, that look as if someone tore them apart or broke their necks. Do you know what strength it would take to do that?" She asked him if he thought she'd done it. "No. But someone must have heard something. We have to close this case and there are no cameras to go on, and all the people there have the same story as you. They don't know anything either."

"And that's my problem how?" He didn't say anything, but she could tell he was pissed off. "Perhaps you should go and find out who the men are and see what they did to make someone so upset with them."

When he walked away, she felt the nudge of Noah in her mind. She wanted to scream at someone, but let out a long breath when he asked her if she was all right.

I can come in there and kill him for you. Or perhaps Trent will want to do that. He is most upset with everyone. Just as his dad was showing up, he took off to the woods. Joe knew that he was upset. He'd told her that he'd come for her after he'd run off some of his anger. *Is he going to be all right, my dear?*

I think he was afraid for me. Noah said that was more than likely it. *He killed the alpha, Noah. There will be consequences for that.*

He will make a great leader, as you will his alpha-bitch. She told him she wasn't so sure about that. *I am. As are the others. TJ is about to burst, he's so happy. I think that the man will be crowing for years to come about this. Does anyone know why he was a part of the robbery?*

Not that I've been made aware of. But then, I'm stuck here in this room with these fools walking all over the evidence. Not that they have much need of it. The men who did it are all dead, and the manager has confessed to everything. She laughed a little. *I don't suppose you had anything to do with that, did you?*

I have no idea what you might be speaking of. If he confessed, he did so because it was good for his soul. If he even has one.

She was released a few minutes later and asked to wait for someone to clear her.

You'll be fine, my dear. Even if I have to take out the entire police force to see that you are.

As the police came in—one standing near her with a gun ready to be brought up at any moment—she reflected on what was going on. Joe could understand what he was doing. There had been a lot of death on his watch, and none of them were taking any chances that they'd get shot as well. When she was released, two of them escorted her to where the Calhouns were, and she sat down on the chair when it was offered to her. She was worried about Trent and hoped he was going to be all right with this.

I'm fine. I'm just...I'll have to run this pack or be killed. Well, not killed, I guess, but we would have to leave the area. It's more than I ever wanted in this life. She told him what Noah had told her. *I saw my dad when I left. Elijah was telling him what had happened. I've never been so afraid in my life. But killing Casey was the only thing my wolf could think to do when we saw him standing over you. I think he planned to try and kill you.*

He did. But you know that he wouldn't have succeeded. He said he knew that. *The manager of the bank had been stealing from here for years. He's confessed to being one of the men in on the robbery, and to have taken some of the cash prior to this. Did you know that?*

Noah said he would take care of it, so that's more than likely the only reason that he confessed. I didn't know what he meant by that, but I really needed to get away and think for a moment. And short of taking you out of there, I had to run. I never expected anything like that from Casey. I mean, he could be a real bastard when he wanted, but to rob the local bank? What did he hope to get from it besides money? Joe knew but for now kept her mouth closed. *I'll be home by the time you are released. Then I'll come and pick you up. I need you.*

Good. I'd like very much for you to take me hard, Trent. Just as soon as you get in the house. He said they'd never make it

127

that far. *Fine with me, so long as I can scream out my releases when you do.*

Joe spoke to the police once more, telling them that all she'd been doing was adding someone to her account when the men came in. No, she didn't know who they were. And she had no idea how they'd been killed. She also told them that she'd not seen anything like a large animal at any time. The officers let her go but told her that they might need to speak to her again. That was fine by her. Joe still wouldn't say a word as to what had really happened.

CHAPTER 8

Max was sitting at his desk when Jefferson came into his office and sat down in the chair across from him. He wanted to tell him that he was too busy to listen to him whine, but didn't. He needed the man more than he might have thought possible only a few days ago. Someone had gotten into his things, and he knew they had his password information on his accounts. All of his accounts. He was still trying to figure out a way to ask him about it when Jefferson finally spoke.

"I spoke to Trent and his brother Elijah this morning." Max glanced at the clock and saw that it was just after eight in the morning. Jefferson must have gotten up early to have done that. Max nodded, then wondered aloud how that had gone. "Fine. Trent really is leaving the company. I have heard different reasons for it, but I think it's the romantic one that I believe. He and his new wife are going to be working on another project that has just fallen into their laps."

When he didn't say more, Max wanted to reach into his top drawer and pull out his gun. There were times, and right now was one of them, that he wished to Christ that he'd never taken this man on as a partner. He was driving him over the edge.

"And what sort of romantic entanglements has he gotten himself into? And what new wife? I had no idea he was even dating anyone seriously. No doubt he thinks that this woman will be the one and only true love of his life and that she'll never cheat or lie to him." Max didn't like the smile that Jefferson wore and wanted to hit him. "Who on earth would want to marry into that family? I mean, they aren't nothing more than a bunch of wolves, if I remember correctly. There is not a woman alive that would want to fuck something like them."

"You'd be surprised." Before Max could ask Jefferson what he meant, the man continued. "He's found his mate. I'm sure you know what that means. Anyway, he's also going to be the leader of their group. Pack, I think they call it. But I'm sure you knew what he was, what his family was, when you went to them about the loan we needed."

"So? You investigate people, too, before you want to work with them. I want to know how this affects our business with him." He'd still not mentioned to Jefferson that Trent had backed out of the deal, and wondered if Trent had told him already. Could be the reason that Jefferson was here now...he was pissed off. Max had a few things to work out, and one of them was getting Noah to give him everything that he wanted. He had a plan in the works right now that might get him more money than the deal that had fallen through with Trent.

"His brother is taking over the business. Elijah Calhoun is the man that I've been dealing with on things, in the event that you wondered. He and I had a long talk, and I think we've reached a deal that will benefit the company." Max started to think things might be turning around for him when he realized what Jefferson said. "You, however, will not be working with me on this or any other project from now on."

"What do you mean? This is just as much my business as it is yours. And besides, I thought we agreed that I'd take care of the banking and you were going to be the one that gathered up the deals for us. I mean, it's been working for us for a while now." Jefferson just stared at him. "You're beginning to piss me off, Jefferson. What the hell has gotten into you? And what is this crap about me not being in on any of the projects?"

"For you it has been working out, hasn't it, Max?" Max glanced at the drawer that held his gun. "I just thought it would be a nice change for me to get to know both sides of the business. And Elijah made it very easy to learn what I needed. You should probably talk to him. After you leave here, that is. He might be able to help you out too."

"Oh, I plan on it. You just stick to what you know best and I'll work with Elijah." He realized how harsh that sounded and cleared his throat before continuing. "Just please let me deal with this part of the business. I feel so useless with the rest, and this is what I do best."

Jefferson said nothing but stared at him. Max had never felt as uncomfortable around this man as he did right now. Something about him was decidedly scary, and Max didn't like it one bit. Jefferson got up to make his way toward the door, and Max was about to call out to him to say he wasn't going anywhere. But Jefferson stopped and turned toward him.

"I'm going to look over some things on the books today. I'm telling you this so in the event that you come looking for me, I won't be in my office. I'm doing it at home. It'll be much easier and with fewer distractions."

Max wanted to tell him he wasn't fucking going to touch the books, but Jefferson smiled at him. "I got them from your office last night. I had a whim to see them and knew that you'd not mind. I mean, we are equal partners, right?"

"Yes. We are." His mind was in a whirl from trying to figure out what else Jefferson had taken from his office. "I don't like that you've been in my things, Jefferson. I'd never do that sort of thing to you, like rummage around in your personal things."

"Wouldn't you?" Again a cryptic message that Max didn't understand. "Anyway, I've got them now, so if you go to look for them or me, you know where they are."

As soon as the door closed behind Jefferson, Max reached into his lower drawer and saw that it was empty. Not just of the things that he'd been keeping there, but he just knew that if he pulled the drawer all the way out, he'd find that his notes were gone as well. All of them. Taking out the drawer, as he'd done a million times, he nearly sobbed when he saw that not only were his notes gone, but there was now a sticky note there. Pulling it off the wooden under-drawer, he read the little note with shaky fingers.

"Safe inspected on today's date." The date of yesterday along with the time was printed in Jefferson's neat handwriting. "An inventory of what was taken is now inside, along with a notarized sheet of what was found."

Max wasn't sure what he was supposed to do now. Not only had Jefferson taken all of the cash that was in the safe, but it looked like he'd taken out Max's passports—all of them—as well as some jewelry that he'd had since he'd taken it from a woman long ago. Max was trying to think of a way to fix this when his phone rang, nearly causing him to cry out. Max had it on the tip of his tongue to tell the person on the other end of the line he was too busy to speak now, but the person started talking first.

"Hello, Benson." His blood seemed to stop moving through his veins at the sound of his name being spoken. "I was wondering if you are able to sleep at nights knowing that the death of a child is on your list of horrible acts. Do you sleep well at night?"

"Who is this? And what are you talking about?" He knew in the back of his mind that engaging with someone on the phone was about as helpful as talking to his walls, but he was upset. "What child?"

"Sydney's baby, of course." Max was glad that he was sitting down, because even sitting he was having a hard time remaining upright. "She was just under three months when you raped her, causing her to not just lose her child but her life as well. Did you know that you are going to regret your actions that night for the rest of your life? Short as it's going to be?"

The line had been dead for some time before he put the handle back in the cradle. Max wasn't sure whether the person on the other end of the line was telling him the truth or not, but he had a feeling that he was. Sydney had been sick a great deal when he'd been trying to pursue her, but she'd never mentioned a child. Leaning back in his chair, the note in his hand forgotten, he wondered if he'd left anything behind when he'd left her chilling body on the floor.

There had been blood, of course. But even now he thought it was from the way he'd taken her. And he had, hard and without any thought to what it did to her. Max had thought a few times over the years that someone would come for him, that the DNA he'd left behind would have been enough. But nothing had occurred over the years, not even a call to ask him where he'd been that night.

Or even what he had done to the brat next door. That had been something Max had thought would come back on him, but it too had supposedly been ignored, as if it had never happened. He'd been pissed...impulsive and pissed off. Something he rarely was nowadays.

He had no idea how long he sat there thinking over what he'd done, how it was coming back for him. For some time after the call, all he could remember thinking about was...well, everything. The money, the safe, the books, Sydney, and the child. The kid next door. Max had to get out of town. Right now. Picking up his phone again, he decided to have some of his other money wired directly to his bank, then he'd leave. Nothing here was worth him going to prison over.

Within minutes the lady at the other end was telling him to hold on, that she needed to contact his bank to make sure that the accounts were ready to receive the funds. When she came back on, he was almost afraid to hear what she had to say.

"Sir, your bank is closed. Until further notice. If you have another account that I can send it to, in another bank, I can certainly send it out today." He asked her why the bank was closed. "I'm not sure, sir. All the person at the other end said was that there were some problems at the bank and that until they got them fixed, the bank was closed for business. I can send the money to that account, but I don't think you'll be able to take it out. Even the local level ATMs are closed, he told me."

"That's not possible. I have money in that bank. You have to tell them that I need my money." She didn't answer him, and he wasn't even sure what she might have said to him anyway. "I need the funds that you're sending to me. Can't you just send them to one of those money places? Or have someone just bring it to me from one of your branches?"

"I'm sorry, sir, but we can only put the money in a bank account. We don't trust those sort of institutions. As for branches, we don't have those in the States either. It's why we are able to collect and keep your money safe without being affected by the laws governing your country." He'd collected his money by simply stealing it, and she was afraid to put his ill-gotten gains in another place for fear of it being stolen? If that wasn't irony, he had no idea what was. "If you have another account at a different bank, we can wire it there."

He hung up on her. Max was in deep shit. He knew that and was pretty sure that if he didn't get out of town soon—like today—he was going to pay dearly for his mistakes. All of them would come back to bite him in the ass now that Jefferson had taken his books. But he had no money, no jewels to cash in, and all his passports were now in the hands of the man he'd been cheating for a very long time. Max didn't like this one bit.

As he headed for his bedroom to start the process of closing down his house, he thought of all the shit that had happened since Noah had made his presence known. What the hell had Max been thinking, keeping things like that in his safe? He wasn't. And now the one person that he had taken on as a partner to make him look good was going to destroy him.

His butler was coming out of his bedroom when he came up the stairs. "Sir." Max nodded at him but said nothing as he just stood there. "There has been a small issue, sir. I'm not sure that you've been made aware of it as yet, but all of your accounts have been closed. The checks that you wrote to us for our weekly wages have been denied. And the grocer and the other services are demanding money that the accounts cannot cover."

"I'm not sure what's going on. I was just informed that the banks are closed. I don't suppose you know what's going on, do you?" Bennington told him about the robbery. "Well, that explains it then."

"No, sir, it does not. The missus and I went to the bank before the robbery and we were told that your accounts, all of them, have been closed by the government. That there are some problems that will not be resolved in the near future. She told us that we were to go and speak to you to have this resolved. Mr. Marshall informed us that you are penniless and that we should leave with whatever goods we can lay our hands on."

"I don't think you have that right. And since when do you steal from me at the word of someone like Jefferson?" Max was pretty sure he had it correct, but he was trying to buy time. Then he realized that Bennington had a small case in his hands. "Are you actually stealing from me?"

"I am taking compensation for wages. As I was told we should do. Unless, of course, you have cash. It is the only form of payment that I'll trust from you from now on." As Bennington started by him, Max reached out to grab him and found himself on the floor. The man had moved so quickly and had him tossed over his shoulder and down that he'd not even had time to react. "Do not presume to touch me again. I do not work for thugs or men that steal from me. Good day, sir."

Max was still laying there when he heard the front door open and close. He did wonder briefly what else they might have taken, but was too upset to care at the moment. If he was in trouble with the government, then it mattered little what was stolen from him now.

~~~

Trent found himself walking around the house just looking at things that he had absolutely no idea what he was looking at. Not that he didn't know the items, but he couldn't have told someone had they asked what he'd looked at to save his life. Things were just going too quickly for him to think beyond the second. He looked behind him when he heard his name called softly.

"Do you like this room?" He looked around the room when Joe asked him. "I do. It's well-lit, and coming in here makes me feel safe. Which is silly, I suppose, since there are more windows than walls really."

"I wouldn't think that Noah could spend a great deal of time in this one. Unless it's dark out." She told him he rarely came in here even if she was here. "Why is that?"

"This is my domain, as he calls it. Somewhere that is all mine." She came more into the room and sat on the fainting couch. He'd seen them before, of course, but only in pictures or movies. "What's bothering you? You're acting like a caged animal, when I know for a fact that you are as free as I am."

"Everything and nothing at the same time. I've talked to the council for this region, and they're very happy with the turn of events concerning Casey and myself. I guess he's been fucking up big time, and they were hoping for someone to come and kill him. Their words, not mine." She nodded, and he moved toward her. Joe was beautiful laying there watching him, and he had a feeling that she was humoring him for some reason. Or she was trying to help him work things out. "My dad is happy that I'm in this position. I thought for sure he'd tell me he'd take it for me, but when I told him what had happened, he said he was happy for me. And you as well."

"Why for me?"

He told her he didn't know and sat on the chair that was across from her. Leaning back, Trent let his mind drift while she said nothing. Then he remembered what he'd been thinking about. "The pack is not without funds, just so you know. I mean, not a great deal, but enough to sustain them for a little while. We've also found out that not only was Casey in on this robbery, but the police were able to attach his name, and those of the other robbers, to a string of other robberies in the area." He closed his eyes as he continued, his body finally feeling slightly relaxed. "His mate told the council and myself that he did it because he could and he was good at it. She seemed to think it was all right for him to do whatever he wanted...he was the pack leader, after all. And the money that he took in the previous robberies had gone to buying some property in another country, as well as several houses. The council is trying to figure out what to do with that."

His mind began the pleasant task of closing down. He'd not been sleeping well, mostly due to the fact that he was worried about everything, but he was staying up later and later just to make love to Joe. Grinning, he wondered if she'd let him shift and chase after her before dinner.

When he woke, the room was dark. Not completely blacked out, but just bright enough from the moon shining into the room for him to see that Joe was no longer on the couch. Stretching as he stood up, he nearly cried out when he realized that he wasn't alone in the room. He sat back down when Noah began speaking.

"I need a favor from you." He told him he'd do anything for him. "Not so hasty, my good man. But this won't cost you overly much. I should like to have a small sampling of your blood. Just to be able to communicate with you and find you should I need to."

"Joe said that when she was in the bank, you couldn't contact her until she reached out to you. Why, do you know?" When Noah didn't answer him, Trent continued. "Casey has been named as one of the robbers yesterday. There is some question as to why he was found naked at the scene, but no one is overly concerned with that. The cameras, as you know, have been replaced and the bank will open in a few more days. No one even mentioned us being there other than the manager, and he's been carted off to jail as well."

"She is your mate." Trent nodded, not sure where the man was headed. "When she became your mate—and I'm only guessing here—my contact with her was severed. Not entirely, because she was able to contact me, but I think that with you there, being her mate, you became a priority to her. I think. It's the reason that I think I was unable to contact her when you told me she was in trouble. I should like to have a small taste of your blood so that in the event that I can't find her, I can talk to you."

"Sounds like…I have no idea. I'm still trying to wrap my head around this house and all the money." They both laughed. "But really, I'm working through this. The money is the most important thing. Not that I'm not thrilled to have it, but it is more than I've ever had. Being the pack alpha was something that I had hoped for someday, so now that I have it, I have some things to work out with actually dealing with it. Having Joe at my side, I think we'll do a great job at it. And as for you wanting my blood? Let's just say as weird shit goes, that doesn't even register as much of a concern."

"You'll do a great job at it. You were born to lead, as was Joe." Trent thought about his first request and told him he was fine with it. "You will never be able to take it back, Trent. I will have your scent as well as be in your mind for the rest of my days."

"As will I with you. I'd like to do a fair exchange. My blood for yours." Trent wasn't sure Noah was going to agree with it, but he smiled and nodded. "Taking your blood into me, will that do anything to me later?"

"To be honest, I hope so." The smile made him a little nervous. "What I have, Joe has; in return, you too have it. Taking my blood might enhance what you have. But for sure? I don't know."

Fair enough, he supposed. As he put out his wrist for the man, several things popped into his head at once. He'd be basically in bed with a vampire. A very old and very powerful one. As Noah's teeth sank into his wrist, Trent thought of something else. Noah was now and would be forever his friend.

"I thank you for that. I think of you as my family as well." Trent nodded and took the wrist of Noah. "I will cut it for you. Someday you might develop fangs, but for now, we'll do it this way."

The blood that was there was dark. And when he pulled it into his body, licking the beads of blood with his tongue, Trent tasted not just the richness but also the strength in it. The power of it raced over his body in a long shuddering race to fill his cells, and Trent felt slightly dizzy. Leaning back in the chair and closing his eyes, he felt the connection immediately.

"I must take my leave." Trent nodded, nearly drunk on the blood. When Noah laughed, Trent looked at him with one eye slightly opened. "You will do very well, my friend. Very well indeed."

The next thing he knew, Trent was waking again. This time it was to Joe sitting on his lap. She smiled at him when he sat up and pulled her into his arms more securely for a long and much needed kiss.

"I missed you too," she told him when he let her up. "I was thinking you were never coming to bed, and I find you here sleeping it off in a chair and not our bed."

"I had a short talk with Noah. And we exchanged blood." She told him she knew that and had felt it. "I figured as much. He is very powerful, isn't he?"

"He is. And now, so are you." As much as he wanted her to explain that, he wanted her naked more. "I think we'd have more fun in the bed."

"Maybe. But for now, I'd like to have you ride me." He helped her to stand and watched her hungrily as she stripped down for him. "Christ, you are so beautiful. And all mine."

When she was naked, he pulled her to him. He had thought to taste her, to eat at her pussy until she was as needy as him. But as soon as he touched her, he felt her need spike, and his wolf moved along his skin. He wanted his mate as well.

"I'm going to shift and let my wolf have you first. If I don't, he's going to distract me when I take you."

As she sat down and spread her thighs by putting them up and over the arms of the chair, Trent nearly took his dick off with his zipper. He didn't move as Joe's fingers slowly slid down her belly to her pussy. His pants were open, his cock freed, and he'd stopped breathing. Watching her pleasure herself, hearing her moan and say his name, Trent knew that if he were to die now, he'd be one happy wolf.

"Hurry. Or do you expect me to do this all on my own?" Her fingers disappeared inside of her. "I want to feel your cock here, Trent. Tell your wolf to hurry or there will be nothing left for him."

Pulling off his pants the rest of the way, he licked her while bent at his waist. Letting his wolf take him, the beast inside of him moved along his skin until Trent the man was no more. His wolf moved closer to her, whining quietly as she spread her nether lips for him.

"Taste me." His wolf moved his head to her and licked her. The taste, Trent knew, was spectacular. And when his wolf licked her again, Trent knew that she was enjoying it. As soon as she came, holding his wolf's head to her, his wolf fucked her with quick, hard strokes with his tongue until she was screaming again.

He took him then, his wolf giving him up so calmly that Trent knew that he'd had his fill. For now anyway. Trent took over where his wolf had stopped. Joe held his head too, holding him there as he ate ravenously at her. Sliding his finger into her, fucking her as his tongue was, cream slid down his hand to his elbow. Still he ate her, drinking as deeply of her as he could. When she jerked his head up, holding him away from his prize, Trent growled low, his need too powerful to be denied.

"Fuck me." He shook his head, tugging on her hand to go back to his feast. "Fuck me now. I need to feel you fill me, Trent. Fuck me."

Standing up, he growled at her to do the same. As soon as she was standing up, her legs wobbly, he turned her to the chair and bent her nearly in half. Pulling her ass to him, Trent plowed her as hard as he could, fucking her like his wolf would have had he been able.

"Come. Let go and come for me." He wasn't sure she understood him, his voice was still so thick with his wolf. When she cried out she was coming, Trent bent over her, pushing her face into the chair cushion, and bit deeply into her shoulder. As soon as she tightened around him, coming again, he let his own climax take him as he sucked on the wound he'd just created.

Tearing into her flesh made his cock fill again. And when she took his arm to her mouth, his wrist exposed for her fangs, Trent fucked her until he was sure that he was going to pass out. The moment her mouth moved over his pounding pulse, he came, screaming out her name as she bit into him. Trent felt his entire world shift and center in a matter of seconds.

CHAPTER 9

Noah opened his eyes. The room was pitch black, but he, like most of his kind, could see movement in the darkest and deepest inkiness. But when someone or something entered his lair, he could see better than at any other time.

Rising up slowly, he kept track of where the human was that had dared to enter his domain. Moving off his bed, lifting himself up by his own magic, he hovered above his bed enough that he not only knew who was there, but also that the man had brought a gun. There was no silver in the casings, nor was there any on the person himself. But there was something—more than likely a stake made of the purest walnut—in the man's hand, held at the ready.

Are you all right? He smiled when he felt the touch of Trent in his mind. *I have no idea what's going on right now, but I can feel something from you. Danger, I guess. My first instincts are to come and save you, but I have a feeling I'd just be in your way.*

I have a visitor in my room. He knew that he should tell the wolf to come to his aid, but for now Noah was going to try and deal with this fool on his own. *I have no idea why*

Max thinks that being here is going to go well for him, but for now I shall see what he has to say. You are not here, are you?

No. We're at my house, packing up my stuff. It was so late when we got finished, we decided to stay here. I'm going to come there and —

Oh no. Don't do that. I have this under control. He has no silver on his person, and the stake he has, while expensive, will not penetrate my flesh. Again, with age comes a great deal of magic, and walnut is something that I have guarded myself against. Noah watched the man knock against an end table and hastily set it to rights. *He's never going to be any good at sneaking the way he's fumbling around in my rooms. Dispatching him will be a great pleasure.*

He wouldn't, of course. There were many reasons why the man would walk out of here on his own, and one of them was that Noah had no idea who he had told about coming here. Not to mention who might be waiting for him to come out when he was finished. Noah was thinking about how best to approach the man when Trent laughed.

Joe said to tell you that he could fall down and break his neck. Trespassing is a horrible offense, and that alone could get him arrested. Noah laughed as well. *We're up now should you need us. And we'll be at the house when you rise tonight, Joe said to tell you.*

Fine, I'll expect you then. For now, I feel I must pay attention to the man here. His stake, while a fine one, can't kill me, as I said, but it will hurt me. He thought of the changes that he'd made to his household, and knew that the couple he'd hired would be most upset with him if there was a mess to clean up. *When you come this evening, bring along your family. I have a need to travel for a while, so I'd like to say goodbye.*

Actually, Noah had been able to ward himself off all sorts of manmade things over the years. Stakes, while capable of killing a younger vampire, wouldn't destroy him. There were a lot of other things that would kill someone younger than him, but he wasn't worried about that. The only thing that he'd been unable to keep himself safe from was olive tree wood. And he didn't smell that on the man now.

Finally, his curiosity got the better of him, and he lowered himself to the floor to confront Max on his grounds. But he did keep himself at a safe distance, just in the event that the man was smarter than anyone thought. Noah thought that was giving the man a great deal of credit where it wasn't deserved. He was in the lair of a vampire.

"You should have a very good reason for being here." His voice was purposely low, and he barely managed to keep himself from laughing when Max not only knocked the end table over and broke the lamp that had been sitting on it, but upended the chair it had been sitting near as well. "Max? Or should I call you Benson? Either way, you had better explain how you got inside of my home."

"Where is she?" Noah asked him who he was talking about. "That woman. Joe, or whatever the hell her name is. I want you to tell me where she is. I know she's at your beck and call. Bring her around to us now. I want to see her."

"With her mate, I would assume." Max looked confused. Turning on the light, Noah waited for both their eyes to adjust before he continued. "You came to my home looking for Joe? Whatever reason you have for wanting her had better be worth your life, because that's what it's going to cost you for being here."

"You think you scare me? Well, you don't. I've come prepared." Noah disarmed the man and moved back to his seat before Max knew what he'd been about. He put the gun on the bed, a safe distance away, and the stake, which was cheaply made, in the wall behind him. It was a show of force, yes, but he'd made his point well, it appeared. As he stood there looking at his empty hands like a moron, Noah took that time to look at Max.

He'd been through a great deal, it appeared. Not only was his suit mussed up, but his hair looked like something had moved into it and built condos. And his tie, usually so straight and clean, now looked as if he'd been using it as a napkin, as well as something to keep his face mopped. The man was a mess, and Noah could smell the fear on him.

"What did you just do?"

Noah said nothing, his mind working out how the man had gotten into his house instead of what he'd done to him.

"I came here to talk to Joe. Where is she? We have business to attend to."

Noah reached into the man's mind none too gently and raped it. He found out a great deal from the search, and the reason he was there in the middle of the night. Sitting down and leaning back in his chair, Noah commanded Max to sit. He did, right on the floor.

"Do you have any idea what I am? I'll save you the trouble of trying to figure it out. I'm a very old and powerful vampire whose lair you just entered. I don't have the energy or the inclination to argue with you on the finer points of breaking and entering, but coming here to kidnap my child is going to get your throat ripped out." Max claimed that people knew where he was. "No one knows where you are, and if you had bothered to tell anyone, no one would care. You are simply on your own. As you have been for quite some time. Now don't lie to me again. I won't tolerate it."

"You claim you're a vampire. And I'm just supposed to believe you. I don't, in the event you care. But my business is with Joe. She owes me." Noah said nothing, knowing exactly what Max thought Joe owed him. "As for kidnapping her, I don't know what you're talking about."

"Of course you do. You think that because you came in here without anyone being the wiser that you can do as you damned well please about getting Joe to go with you. She's told you no before, Benson or Max or whatever the hell you're calling yourself now, and I'm sure she will do so again. Joe has a mate now." Noah knew that, although Max said that his business was with Joe, his intentions were to take her from Noah and use her to finance his way to Europe to get to his funds. "The money is gone, you know. All of it. I could tell you where it's gone to, but I won't. I think it will be more fun for all those involved for you to find out on your own."

"What do you mean it's all gone? I have millions of dollars in those accounts, and I aim to get it. Once you pay me for getting Joe back, I'm going to get out of here and never return." He was never going to return—he had that much right—but as for the money, not only was it gone, it had been put into a nice fund for the victims of senseless crimes. "Tell Joe to get her ass down here and I'll be on my way."

"Do you seriously think that I'd just call her down to my lair for you to kidnap?" Max looked confused again. "I told you already, she's not here. She and her mate have gone to their own home and shan't be returning."

"Shan't? What the hell does that mean?" Noah started to explain. "I don't really care. And you make her come with me. I need to get out of here. Someone has been calling me and saying things that…well, I don't care for it. So I'm not telling you again to get that bitch down here."

"You've been getting calls? About what?" Noah didn't know what Jefferson was doing about calls, but apparently it was working. Max was about as scared as he'd ever seen a human be. "Someone has been haunting you, Max? About what deed this time? I'm sure there are plenty to choose from."

"Never you mind. None of them are true, but they have to stop, and they will as soon as you pay me to give you back Joe." Max sat there looking at Noah expectantly. "Well? When are you going to call her to me?"

"I'm not, and I have no idea why you think I would. The police are looking for you." Noah had no idea if they were or not, but it got a reaction from Max. "Yes, they're wondering about a murder that happened long ago. A woman had been living alone when you were there. If I remember correctly, you knew her quite well."

"Cindy? So what about her? No one is going to miss a tramp like her. I did her family a favor by doing what I did. Or if you're talking about Addie Mae, then that's another one that no one cares about." Noah said nothing, but did reach out to Trent again to tell him the names of the two women. "I've been waiting here patiently, Noah. Where is Joe?"

"Gone. And I was referring to Sydney Carlin. You remember her, don't you, Max?" Max's face paled and he stiffened. "I can see that we've touched on a memory. Is that who you've getting calls about? Poor Sydney, who you raped and left dead on her living room floor? Why? Because she wouldn't give you what you wanted?"

"That was all your fault and you know it. She was mine and you told her to stay away from me, that I wasn't good enough." Noah asked him how it was even possible that it was Noah's fault. "You told her to make me look bad, and that I was a crook. Then you had her family come after me. Did you know that they ran me out of town?"

"Sydney had no family, Max. Whoever ran you out of town wasn't her family. Perhaps it was the people who liked her and not you. But you had to go and kill her, didn't you? For no other reason than you'd been found out." Max stood up then and began pacing across Noah's room, and Noah let him. The man was obviously unhinged, and Noah was going to get as much information as he could out of him before he let him go. "What about her haunts you so much? Could it be that she was going to have a child and you murdered it as well?"

"It wasn't mine." That sounded to Noah like a justification rather than a confession. "All she had to do was marry me and then give me all her money. It's not like she spent any of it. What the hell did she think she was going to do with it?"

"There was no money." Max told him he lied. "No, I don't lie, and there was no money to speak of. She was living in the brownstone that belonged to another, and she was working for pennies a day, almost, just to keep food in her belly. The only thing she had in her whole life was her goodness, and you took that from her."

Max continued to pace. Noah told Trent to contact Jefferson and let him know that Max was running scared. It was time the man was brought down, and he wanted Jefferson to be the one to do it.

All right. But are you okay? Max is off his rocker, his butler said. The guy that works for you, Michael I think Joe said, is a friend of his, and he said that in order to get their money, they took some things of value from the home. There's not much there, I guess. He'd have to have a talk with Michael and see what else his friend said. *Oh, and Joe said to tell you that you should also mention Benny by name. Not anything about him, but just that Benny misses his friend.*

Good idea. Keep him on his toes until Jefferson gets here. Noah asked if they were coming there. *I think you should both stay where you are. It's a lovely night. You should go out in the woods with your lovely mate.*

We're there now. Noah nearly laughed at the man's tone, like he'd had his candy taken from him. *She's very worried about you.*

Tell her that I'm fine. And he was too. *All right. I have to lay groundwork before Jefferson comes and saves the day. You two have a lovely evening. I shall speak with you both tomorrow.*

"You've never gotten in touch with Joe. I need her to get her ass down here and help me out. It's the least you can do for me. The two of you have been fucking me over for years, and now it's time I got a little payback." Noah asked Max how he thought he owed him anything. "You shouldn't have done that to me. I would have been a very rich man had you just kept your nose out of my business."

"Benny misses her too, you know." Max's entire demeanor changed. He'd been pacing back and forth, his body seemingly lax in his movements, but now he was stiff as a rail and his face was blood red. "You do remember him, don't you? The neighbor of the woman you raped and murdered."

"That brat caused me more trouble than you did." Before Noah could ask him how, he continued as if he'd been waiting for a chance to spill his guts to someone. "Always right there. Peeking around the corner when I was trying to get her to open the fucking door or to come out when I told her. He was forever telling me that she wasn't home, when I knew that she was. I had to have him hurt a few times just so that I could go out on a date with Sydney."

"You never dated Sydney. The one time you were seen with her was when she was out with someone else and you came and pushed your way into her table. What did you do to young Benny?" He could feel his anger taking control. One thing that Noah always prided himself on was his control, but he was losing it now. "Tell me."

The compulsion took Max to the floor, and Noah had to back off a little or kill him. As he lay there screaming in pain Noah pushed just a little harder. Finally, when his nose and ears started to bleed, Max spoke.

"I had him tied up and raped." Noah staggered back. "The fucking little shit was driving me crazy and keeping me from getting any from her. So I had him get a little of his own. When you all had me run out of town, it took every penny I had to get back at him. And now that he's taken care of, I'm working on you. Bring Joe to me now."

Noah's anger was profound. Just as he was lifting his hands up to deal with Max, Noah heard someone behind him. Turning to see the man there, he knew in that moment that whatever Jefferson had planned for Max, it was going to be no more than he deserved.

"Hello, Benson. Remember me? I'm Benny Gibson." The howling started. Not from Jefferson but from Max. His need to get up from the floor to harm the younger man was making him sicker. Noah looked at the two of them and went to the door. This was out of his hands.

~~~

Joe sat on the tree limb and waited for Trent. He'd gone to get their clothing and told her to stay where she was. To be honest, she wasn't sure she could go far anyway…he'd worn her out again. Noah had told her what had happened to Benny as a boy.

"Noah is at the cabin now." She nodded, telling Trent that she'd spoken to him as well. He handed her her pants and she began the process of pulling them on while he watched. "He said that he left the two of them in his house. Do you suppose that Jefferson will kill Max?"

"No. I don't know why I don't think so, but I just don't think that Jefferson has it in him. But then I had no idea what Max had had done to him when he was a child. Had I known…had I known, Max wouldn't have been a threat to us all these years." Trent handed her his shirt, and she pulled it on and sat back down on the wood with him. "So much has happened since I met you. I'm looking forward to things being normal. Do you think it will be?"

He said he didn't think so. "But we have the cabin to run to when things get bad. Oh, and Scott is going to buy my house, and Mom and Dad are going to help him get some furniture. I should have taken more care to get things for it, but I was never really comfortable there. And Elijah has three new clients that will help him save his money for buying me out. So while they're not normal, they're looking better, don't you think?"

"You did tell him that it wasn't necessary that he buy the house from you, didn't you?" He said that he had, but Scott wanted to own it, not be given it. "Are all you Calhoun men so stubborn? Or is it just you boys?"

"Have you met my parents at all? I mean, they are the very definition of stubbornness. I'm pretty sure we got it honest." He sat down on the ground in front of her and smiled. "I love you, Joe."

"I love you too. Very much so. I don't know what I would have done had you not come into my life." He said that she would have survived. "Yes, but I'd not be happy. I don't think I ever was. Safe, yes. Even glad to have someone in my life like Noah, but happy was something that I never allowed myself to be. It was easier to just be ready for someone to disappoint me rather than give my heart to them."

"When I was younger, about twelve, my dad and I went up to the cabin. Just the two of us. Anyway, while there, Dad told me about meeting my mate and falling in love. He said that it would change me in ways that I'd never be able to comprehend then, but that when I grew up and found her, I would remember his words and know that he was telling me the truth." Joe started laughing. She had no idea why, but she bet that TJ had told his son the honest truth and scared his oldest boy. "He said that I'd have to learn to share my things, pick up after myself, and to know that nothing that I owned before was going to be mine again. All that I had would be hers, and I'd willingly give it to her."

"What did you say to that?" Trent took her hand in his, the one that had his family ring on it, and kissed it. When he pulled her down to the ground with him, holding her tightly in his arms, she kissed his arm and let him hold her. "Trent? What did you say to him?"

"I told him that if I ever found a girl that wanted to take my stuff, I'd run fast in the other direction and never look back. Mind you, all that I owned at the time was a stack of girly magazines that I was sure that no one knew about, a fifty-cent piece that my great-grandda gave me when I was eight, and two comic books that I treasured more than I did my own family. So sharing my wealth seemed the most ludicrous thing in the world to me."

She turned in his arms and looked up at him. He was leaning his head on his hand and had the most boyishly charming look on his face. Tracing his lips with her fingers, she thought of all the times that she'd been alone, really alone, and wondered if she'd ever want that again.

"TJ told me that when we take over the pack, we'll have to be stern and hard on them at first. To show them that we are there to help, but not to be run over. But we'd have to be gentle, too, as they have had a hard time with their lives since Casey took over." Trent nodded. "I don't know how to be a pack alpha with you. I know very little of your kind, and other than the few things that your mother told me about being a wolf in a pack, I don't know all the rules yet."

"I know. Mom is looking for a charter book. I'm not sure who wrote it or when, but I know that there is one. As for being a pack alpha with me, you're going to be perfect at it. I have all the faith in the world in you." She started to ask him why, but he kissed her on the mouth and sat up. "There is someone coming. Pack if I don't miss my bet. Just stand beside me and we'll see what we can figure out for them."

As soon as she saw the three men, she knew that there was going to be trouble. Not sure what it was, she felt the need to protect Trent from them, but knew that to do so would make him look less in charge and more like a henpecked man. Instead, she stood at his side while the men spoke.

"We been told you're in charge." Neither of them spoke, and Trent took her hand in his and gave her a tight, quick squeeze. "Did you know that there aren't any jobs for us in the pack? No jobs means we have to go elsewhere to find them. We're wanting you to let us go."

"All right. You're free to go." None of the three men moved, but they did look confused. "I'm not going to hold anyone here that doesn't want to be here. I have plans to bring jobs to the pack and the area, but if you think you can do better elsewhere, then by all means go ahead and pack up your family and go."

"We was thinking we'd leave them here while we looked." The second man who spoke looked like he was sneering at them. "You can take them on like they was your own. That's what a pack master does when his men need to find work."

"No. You leave them behind and I'm well within my rights to kill them all." The first man looked at his buddy but didn't comment. "It might be better for them if you take them now in the event that when you find work, you find a pack that will put up with your bullshit. I don't have time to explain to the council that I've had to kill off three families right away. As I said, I have plans for jobs, but I won't have time to work on that when taking care of a family that you're basically abandoning."

"What do you think of this? Your mate killing off women and babies without a care in the world. You gonna let him do that?" The third man pointed at her when he spoke. "You gonna just let him kill our families when we leave? You got any kind of heart in you that would allow a man to kill off a family?"

"First of all, I don't appreciate you trying to pit me against my mate and your alpha. And, really, did you expect less of him? You've known him his entire life. And his family. Did you really think that they'd not follow the rules and regulations of pack law because you think there is something better out there?" The man flushed a little, and she took a step toward him when he lowered his head. "When you speak to me, you look me in the eye. And while you're at it, you straighten up and act like a man about this. Because as surely as we're all standing here, you know what the law states. You thought when you came here that he'd beg you to stay, that he'd offer you just about anything to keep his pack the way it is. It won't be the same, not so long as Trent is in charge. There will be jobs here, so if you want to leave, that's up to you. But you leave one member of your family, and I will help him kill them."

She wouldn't, and she was sure that Trent wouldn't either. But they had to do this, make a stand against bullies, or they'd do this to them forever. And forever for them was just that. A very long time to be pack masters of this group.

"You ain't no better than Casey was."

Before she could think about it too much, Joe slapped the man, hard enough to knock him back into his buddies. When he started to rise up, she pointed her finger at him and he stilled. Her power nearly vibrated off the end of her finger, and she waited to see if she'd have to use it on him. When he didn't move, she spoke in a low hard voice to him.

"Move and I will tear your head off. If you think I can't, then say something like that to us again." He sat down, then curled into a fetal position. When she looked at the other two men, they were bowing as well. Joe looked at Trent, not really sure what was going on. He just winked at her before turning to the three men.

"You boys get back to your homes and stay there until you hear from me. In the meantime, I want you to pull out your pack laws and read them over. A great deal will depend on you knowing them well." After they left, Trent looked at her and smiled. "Christ. What were you just telling me about not being any good at this? You nearly made them wet themselves. Me too, as a matter of fact."

"He insulted us." Trent nodded and pulled her to his body. "I don't think I like being in charge. It sort of goes to your head for a few seconds."

"So long as you know who's in charge at home." She told him he could be in charge everywhere. "No, darling, it's you. You're in charge at home. I love you."

As they made their way back to his house, she wondered what was in store for them now. Something good, she hoped. She wanted a good thing to come their way.

CHAPTER 10

Jefferson was sitting in the lobby of the building waiting for one of the Calhoun men to show up. He wanted to talk to Trent alone, but he knew that he was asking a great deal of the family. Jefferson really wasn't sure what he was going to say to Trent — there was plenty to tell him — but he had to talk to the man, and soon.

Yesterday had not been one of his better days. Which he supposed was an understatement. He'd done things yesterday and well into this morning that would…it would get him killed. By electrocution, if the state was still doing that.

When he heard the door open, he and the secretary who had been coming in when he'd gotten there stood up. Jefferson was ready. For what, he really wasn't sure. He looked at the man and wondered if he'd made the right decision in coming here before turning himself in.

"Mr. Marshall. I wasn't expecting you." He knew this Calhoun…it was Elijah. Not Trent who he'd hoped to speak to. "If you want to see Trent, I'm sorry. My brother no longer works here, but he is coming in this morning if you want to talk to him. He won't be too long."

"I do." He sat down, knowing that if he left now, he'd not return. "I'll just wait right here. He won't have to hurry on my account. I just...I would very much like to speak to him, please."

"He's coming in soon to set up his new digs for his other job. I'm not sure how long that'll be. My dad and he are having a breakfast meeting with the council right now. I'm sorry, but had I known you were coming in, I could have let him know."

Jefferson told him it was fine and he'd wait. He could hear the pride in Elijah's voice about his brother and his new job. He had always thought the men in the Calhoun family were close, but thought now that perhaps that was an understatement. Jefferson had never had any siblings, and had wished when he was younger that he'd had a couple. But now, all he could think about was how he'd just shamed his entire family name.

"Would you like something to drink?"

Alcohol came to mind, but he only shook his head. The things he'd done last night were.... He looked down at his hands and could see a spot of blood on his nail. Picking at it until it was gone, he looked up when the door opened. Not them. Not the man he wanted to talk to.

Max had been curled into a ball when Jefferson had come into the room last night. Noah had been there, of course—it was his house—but the fact that Max had been telling Noah what he'd done to Jefferson had brought out his temper. And Jefferson had never been very good at holding onto his temper. It wasn't as if Max was bragging about it, but almost like he was being forced to tell. It wasn't until this morning that Jefferson had figured it out. He was being forced to talk. Looking at the briefcase next to him, he was also glad that he'd not been asked what was in it. He had to talk to Trent.

The briefcase held his will, what cash he had on him and in his house, as well as the deed to all his properties. He wanted Trent to have it. He knew the man didn't really need it, but there was no one for him to leave it to and he liked the man a great deal. There was also a confession of what he'd done to get to Max, as well as the entire layout of the plan to bring the man down. Also, there were pictures of the body. Max's body.

The things he'd done to the man…the way his rage, let go when Jefferson realized that he no longer cared what happened to him, had torn the man to shreds. Some of the things that he'd done, the way his body had been covered in blood and other things, had made Jefferson sick, so much so that he'd gone into the bathroom and thrown up for twenty minutes. Until there was nothing left in his belly but air. Even then, Jefferson had lain on the cold tile floor of Noah's bathroom and sobbed at what he'd done.

Taking clothing from Noah's own dresser, Jefferson had taken a long hot shower then, scrubbing his body until it burned, and then dressed in the smaller clothing. He stuffed his clothing in the trash can in the bathroom as he left. Jefferson wondered what Noah had thought about coming home to—

"Jefferson?" He looked up, glad to be pulled from what he'd been thinking about when someone said his name. Trent was there. He looked…well, the man always looked put together to him. Jefferson was not really sure what that meant, but it suited Trent more than he could have explained to someone. Standing up, Jefferson pulled him into his arms for a tight and desperately needed hug. When it was returned, Jefferson started to sob like a small boy, his knees weaker from the relief of it until he had to be pulled up or fall on his face. "Come on now. Let's get you in my office. You can tell me what's the matter."

"Your brother said you didn't work here. I'm terribly sorry to have come here, but I didn't know where else to go. Or who to talk to. I've done something horrible." Trent told him he was going to keep an office here for other reasons, but no, he didn't work for the firm any longer. He asked Jefferson if he needed something. "No, I need to just give you something and not take up any of your time. You've been really kind to me, and I—"

"Nonsense. Come on now. We'll sit in here and you can tell me what has you so upset. Tell me what has you thinking you did something horrible. I'm sure you didn't. Tell me."

He really wanted to. Jefferson wanted to talk to this man more than he did anyone. There was something about him, calming and so strong, that Jefferson knew that if anyone could help him, this man could. Not that Jefferson thought that he'd use the help, but he knew it was there all the same.

"Max is dead." He waited for Trent to ask him what he'd done, but he only nodded. The other man—he thought it was Trent's father—sat down in one of the wingback chairs that sat near the desk and smiled at him. Trent was in the other one, and Jefferson was sitting on the couch. "I killed him. Last night. I killed Max Ford. I was at Noah's house when it happened. I'm sure the man is very upset with me for leaving such a...it was a mess there, and I just left it. I have a note for him. And some money to have it cleaned up. I'm not sure if...if he knows anyone that does that sort of thing. On the television there is always a firm that can do that for—"

"Did he hurt you? Did Max hurt you in anyway? I want to see it if he did." Jefferson stood up, not even sure why that was important, and pulled up his shirt to show Trent when he asked. Pulling off the gauze hurt…it was sticking to the dried blood less and less, but it was still painful. He knew the cut along his belly was bad, but he'd done the best he could to stitch it up. He'd found some old pain pills from when he had a tooth extracted and took those. They barely dulled the pain, and today the pain was making breathing and moving most difficult. "Let me have Sandra get some medical supplies, and we'll see if we can fix that up better for you. Anywhere else?"

"My back. I'm not sure what he did to me there. I tried to see it…did you hear what I said? I killed Max." Trent nodded and went to the door, and spoke quietly to the women still out there. Jefferson looked at TJ, who was staring at him sadly. "I don't think he understands what I've done."

"He does. Probably more than you do. Just let him help you. And don't worry about Noah. I'm sure he's got it all taken care of too." Jefferson nodded and sat back down. He knew what he'd done; these men did not. "Jefferson? We'll help you get through this."

Nodding again, he knew that he wasn't getting through anything. Max's death had been well planned, and he'd done it. From the moment he'd hatched this plan—the second Max had killed Sydney—Jefferson had known that he was going to kill Max. The man had deserved it, that was for sure. But the police should have taken care of it.

When Trent came back in and sat down, Jefferson asked for a glass of water. His mouth was dry now, and the story he had to tell was long and horrific. TJ got up to get the water and handed it to him without a word. When he put his heavy hand on his shoulder, Jefferson felt the overwhelming need to cry again. Instead, he took a long pull on the water bottle and looked at the floor.

"When I was sixteen," he said, still looking at the floor, "Sydney Carlin moved in next door to us. My family owned the block, you see, and we would usually rent out one or two of the buildings when someone needed a place to stay. My dad liked her a great deal. She was friendly, sharp, and my mom and she would go on girly things together. Sydney had dinner at my home, sat with us, and watched television when she could. She was my first and only true love. We were friends, she and I. I could tell her just about anything, and I did. My life, I thought, was perfect. Then about a year later, Max came around. I suppose he'd always been there, in the background of things. I never noticed him or didn't take notice of him until a few months later. That was when Sydney told me she was going to have a baby." Trent asked him if she'd ever told him who it belonged to. "No. She only said it had been a mistake and that she was going to give it up. That she was in no position to care for it. I know that now, but back then I thought I could be her knight in shining armor. I could barely keep my own room clean...I have no idea how I thought I'd care for a woman and her child. I wanted to...I was only seventeen and thought that I was deeply in love with her, but I told her that I'd help her. She was so kind to me about it, telling me that I had to grow up and find myself a wife and have my own children. Sadly for me, it never happened."

"The medical examiner only mentioned there was a child, and that she'd lost it upon death. I know that it was a few years ago, but there was never any mention of how she'd been killed either." Jefferson told Trent that he knew that. It was what he'd asked his father to do for him, and he'd told them what else he'd done for her. "Your father stopped the investigation?"

"Oh no. Not that. I just asked Dad to not mention the baby or how she was found. I mean, we never had anything to do with the police never finding who murdered her. I knew, but after what happened later, I could never bring myself to…I'll explain in a moment. But when she died, my father told the coroner that there was no reason to shame such a girl. And that her parents, if they were out there, wouldn't need to know about that either. My father agreed with me, saying that if it were his daughter, he'd not want to know that he'd lost a grandchild as well." Trent nodded. "As far as I've been able to find, there really wasn't anyone left to mourn her but myself. Her parents never came forward, and there was no one that came about the baby either. I don't know that he, whoever he was, had any knowledge of the child. She never dated when she lived in the brownstone. But she really was a very nice woman. And I did love her."

"Of course you did. From all accounts, she was a good person and didn't deserve to die the way she did. But I'd like for you to explain what you meant about explaining something to us. What happened to you, Jefferson?" Jefferson looked at TJ. "You said that something happened later. I'd like to know what that was, please."

"Max—he went by Benson back then—hated me. I guess I didn't really blame him, but I really didn't care. Still don't, not really. He was forever hanging around the building that Sydney lived in and banging on her doors at all hours of the day and night. I would wait for him, you see. Run him off by telling him I was calling the cops. They would show up and he'd be gone, but Sydney would tell them what he'd done if she was home. Or my parents would. I couldn't ever find a police report that was filed about it, but I'm sure that Max knew it was me." Jefferson glanced at the two men, then looked at the floor again. "I became a watchdog for her. Helping her hide out when he came around, warning her when I'd see him coming up the street. When he'd hang around her door, I'd sneak out the other door and go and tell her he was there. I tried my best to keep them apart. Even Noah had come by a few times, and I would keep him away as well. But I found out that all he wanted was her friendship, much in the same way I did. He told me that he just liked her and that he'd never cause her any harm. I believed him."

Neither of them said anything to him. He needed a moment and sat still on the couch before he could talk about her death. Max had killed her. And Jefferson was more than likely the only one in the world that really knew the whole story.

"She'd been at work all day and had invited me over for dinner when she got home. My dad was working, and my mom was at some function that night, so I said yes. Sydney and I would hang out together sometimes when they were gone at night. It wasn't often, but we had a good time together. Anyway, I'd gone home to get something that I wanted her to see. She was encouraging me to go to college and become a better man. But before I returned, Max had gotten into the apartment. It was my fault." Trent asked him how it was his fault. "I left the door opened so that I could return without her having to come and unlock the door for me. She was in the kitchen when I left, making us a bowl of popcorn to share while we watched a movie. It was how he got in and behind her. Max was right there, and I did nothing to help her. Nothing at all."

"You said that you saw him kill her. Is that right?" TJ asked. He nodded "What do you think you might have done to save her, Jefferson? Like we told you before, he would have killed you as well, and then he would have gotten off Scott free. Doing what you did, you might well have saved a great many other lives."

"Perhaps. But I still blame myself for her death. From the moment he knocked her to the floor with his fist to.... I was gone longer than I'd thought. I found a couple of things that I wanted to take back to show her, but when I got there, he was.... I thought she was on the phone with someone at first." Jefferson got up to pace. "He hit her, as I said, punched her in the face hard enough to knock her down. She hit her head on the fireplace, and I thought he'd just leave. But he didn't. He...he tore her underthings off and raped her." Jefferson closed his eyes as the image took shape in his head. He had never forgotten it...never went a day or night without thinking about it. "It took me a few seconds to realize that she was dead when he'd finished. He'd covered her face up with a pillow and was holding it down while he...while he took her. When Max stood up, his body naked from the waist down, he stood over her, laughing. I was positive he had no idea that he'd killed her."

He ended his walk by the window that looked out over the tree-lined street behind the building. It was a lovely park area. The trees were dark against the light of the grass. There was a little boy running with a puppy, laughing. Jefferson didn't bother looking behind him as he continued. The scene in front of him was so surreal that he watched it instead of thinking about the words that flowed from his mouth.

"He yelled at her, screamed really, telling her that she got no less than she deserved for tossing him away. He mentioned money too, how she'd kept it from him, and that's what got her killed. When her blood—and by then there was quite a bit of it on the floor—touched his shoes, he kicked out at her, and screamed at her that it was all her fault again." Jefferson could almost hear him telling her that she was nothing to him, that she should have just given him what he wanted and she would have died more quickly. "Max was going to kill her anyway, I figured out then. No matter what she'd done, he would have killed her. After she agreed to marry him and he got whatever it was he thought that she was holding from him. I don't know what he thought she had, but I think he was under the impression that she had money, and a great deal of it."

"He'd done it before. Not raping anyone so far as we know, but marrying for money, then killing his wife off. Three times that we can find so far. It was always a younger woman that had been left a fortune. Randal found at least two more since Sydney's death, and one prior to it." He knew that as well and told Trent that. "I was sure you did. But I wanted you to know in the event that you didn't. Max wasn't going to just go away. You had no way of knowing that then. Neither did Noah."

"He was a monster. Even after all of that, he continued to be one. I guess since I begged my parents not to...not to tell the police what he had done to me later, I sort of gave him the access to others. I didn't...I was a kid. Not a good excuse, but all I had back then. I was seventeen, overweight, and a nerd. I guess my pride was what I was thinking about then." He watched the young boy in the park playing with the dog as he continued with his part in the story that had gotten Max killed.

"A few weeks after she was killed, I was home alone again. My grief was profound, and I had taken to staying at home even when my parents would go out. I was hiding, I guess, trying to deal with the murder and that I'd done nothing to help her. The knock at my door never…it never occurred to me not to open the door, but when I did...." He shivered when he thought of what had happened next. "There were seven of them. Big men with Halloween masks on their faces and their shirts off. As soon as the door was open, after they shoved their way into my home, they started hitting me. I fought back, but I was no match against them and their size, and I was alone too. Then when I was down — and it hadn't been easy for any of them — they nailed nails in the floor with a nail gun. They had come prepared, was all my mind was working on. As I was tied to the floor by tying my hands above my head and wrapping the rope around the nails, they laughed and told me I was going to enjoy this and that they would, too, if I didn't. After I could no longer get to them to hit back, tape was put across my mouth after a wad of something dirty was put into my mouth to gag me. Then they did the same to my feet, tying me there as if I was nothing. I suppose to them I was just that. Nothing. After they beat me, kicking me to the point where I was sure I was going to die, they stripped off my clothing and each of them raped me."

He remembered it vividly. They'd taken turns with him, each man tearing into him while the others continued to laugh and joke about how much fun they were having. One of them had even taken him into his mouth, making him sick to his stomach even then. And when they were done, they untied him and left him there, his body beaten, bruised, and broken.

"I never had sex after...I'm sure that it's not called sex, what they did to me. But after that I was never able to let anyone touch me like that again. Then after a while, I never even tried." He leaned his head against the cool glass. "My mother found me there, bloodied and bruised, after they left. My father came in next, outraged that someone had done this to me. In our own home. It was everything I could do...I begged them never to tell anyone. I didn't even want the police to know. At that time, in that small frame of time, I thought it was just a random act, that I'd just happened to be in the wrong place at the wrong time."

"When did you figure out it had been Max?" Trent's voice was soft, but Jefferson heard him. "He did tell you, right? I can't see him just letting you think that you were the victim of a random house invasion." Jefferson wished that was all it had been, but he really appreciated Trent not saying "rape." It was hard enough for him to say it, but to hear it from someone else was too much.

"Yes. He told me, took a great deal of pride in it, I think, that he'd hurt me like he had. About a week later, I get this card in the mailbox. I had no idea who it might have been from. There was no return address, not even a postmark or stamp. But it was him. On the front there was a picture of a young boy peeking in the window of a candy store. But he'd changed all the cakes to erect penises and pictures of bottoms. When I opened it, he asked me if I enjoyed my little fun, and that he thought of me often when he saw the men who had done it for him. He'd done it, he told me, because since I'd kept him from getting his piece of ass, he wanted to make sure that I had fun with mine. Then he signed it, 'Love Benson.' I kept it. It's there with the rest of the things I wanted you to have. I don't know what you can do with it, but I brought it."

Jefferson felt relieved and overwhelmed at the same time. He was talked out, his body having spewed the story…and that was what it felt like to him. He knew that he could die in peace. That going to the police station now would be an end to this nightmare that had been long in coming.

"Jefferson?"

He turned to look at Trent and realized that at some point TJ had left them. He was more than likely sickened by what Jefferson had done. He knew that he would be if he'd heard this story. And neither of them knew the worst of it…how he'd not just planned Max's death, but his own as well, and in the last moments had chickened out of that as well.

"Come and have a seat. There's a doctor friend of mine here that wants to make sure you're all right."

Nodding, he made his way to the chair again and sat. He had no idea how long he'd been standing there, just staring out the window, but the doctor came in and had him lay out on the couch. He was gentle with him, but Jefferson still had to brace himself for each touch. It wasn't until he was asked if he wanted anything for pain that he looked over at Trent again.

"Why are you doing this for me?" Trent told him that he was hurt and needed it. "No, I don't mean that. Although I really appreciate it, you really have no need to do this for me. I'm sure that once I'm in prison, they'll take care of me."

Trent nodded at the doctor, and Jefferson felt the small pinch of a needle entering his arm. In seconds he was floating, and a few seconds more he was having difficulty holding his eyes open. But he looked at Trent again, asking him again why he was helping him.

Trent smiled before answering. "Because you're a good man who was dealt a shitty hand. Rest now, Jefferson. We'll talk again when you wake."

Jefferson tried to fight it, the drug that was racing though his body like a freight train. But he didn't have it in him, and in the end, he faded out.

~~~

"There won't be any charges brought against Jefferson. Not now or ever. As far as anyone is concerned, Max Ford didn't exist, and there are no traces of him to be found anywhere near Jefferson or Noah's houses." Joe nodded as Trent continued. "Noah kindly took care of the remains for him. Jefferson killed him with a great deal of rage. I'm pretty sure that Noah will be finding parts of him throughout the house for the next several years."

"He's selling the house. Noah said that he and the staff are going to find somewhere quiet to live, and I guess Jefferson is going to go and stay with him. Not as his day walker, but as his friend. They've become very close over the last several days." Trent knew and he told her he thought it was good for them both. "I think so too. Jefferson is seeing a friend of Noah's. A doctor. He needs to talk to someone that has no vested interest in what he's done, and Noah was agreeing too much with what he'd done. The doctor will listen and not cheer him on as Noah had been doing."

"There are those that would want to hurt Jefferson for what he's done. Others might be glad to shake his hand. But it's doubtful anyone will completely understand what he's gone through with this." Joe didn't think she would either after Trent had told her the rest of Jefferson's story. "Noah said he could make him forget it all, but he's a little afraid that it would ruin him. Those events, horrific as they were, made him what he is today. A good man."

"I hope you don't mind, but I've invited Jefferson to come and help me out on a few projects that I'm working on. He has computer skills that will help me out. Also, I don't know if you know this or not, but your brother Tanner is out of work. He went to an interview with a friend of Noah's to work as a waiter in a restaurant the other day." Trent asked her if he needed anything. "Noah is going to hire him as his attorney. I did it before for him, but Tanner might be better suited to it now that we are together. Besides, I think that Tanner needs this more than he thinks. Not just a job, but a feeling of self-worth. He's very…I was going to say depressed, but I think it's more that he has lost his confidence somewhere along the line."

"I don't know…I've always thought of Tanner as having his shit together more than the rest of us." She said he hid it well. "I guess so. I hope he takes on the job then. Noah is a good man, and he could do no better than to have you and Tanner watching out for him."

She paced the room, then sat down only to hop up again. Trent asked her what she was doing. "I'm nervous, if you want to know the truth. What if they hate me? This is the first time I've ever been a pack-mistress."

"It's pack-bitch, and no one could ever hate you. You're going to be just fine. And as many people as you've talked to this week, I'm reasonably sure that you've met them all at some point." She had been getting out a lot this week. It was that or hide away. Nerves tended to do that to her. "Mom said to tell you that she made your favorite cookies for the cookout, and has hidden some away for you for later."

"She makes the best pumpkin cookies I've ever had." They both sat down. "Did you see to those men from the other day, the ones I was telling you about? They really do need some work, and I told them that we'd find something until the new jobs you have coming in are set. When do you think that will be?"

"I did take care of them. They're now working for Elijah, and two more have gone to work with Dad. He's getting the three buildings downtown set up for several businesses. Mostly pack, but there will be others in it too. Dad is very proud that you asked him to help out. As for the new business, that's working along nicely too. It was great of Noah to put in a manufacturing plant here instead of in another state. That's going to help out a lot of people around here."

Joe just waved him off, thinking about the two men that she'd come to love very much. Trent's dad was going around like he'd been asked to be president or something, and Noah was having the time of his life.

Trent continued talking about other projects she'd been working on. "The two women that make those quilts are going to rent some of the space in the building and open a shop. They're not sure that they'll sell their wares or not, but they want to teach younger people how to make them before the art is lost. Did you have anything to do with that?"

"Maybe. I've spoken to a great many people, as you've pointed out. And a lot of them are very talented." Too many people, she thought now. And they all knew her well enough to come by for a little chat at the house when they were there. Joe had never been very good at chatting, but now it seemed she was doing it constantly. "Your mom is conspiring against me too."

"My mom? I don't think...what did she do? And if you're referring to her having my baby bed delivered to the cabin, I told her to stop that. She can be pushy." That had embarrassed her as well. During one of her chats, it had been delivered and set up in one of the spare rooms. "She does love you a great deal."

"I love her too. But I was talking about her telling everyone that I was a whiz at investments. I don't know anything but what I like." Trent said nothing as he finished dressing. She'd been ready for over an hour while he'd been out dealing with some last minute things that had come up. "I can't stop people from asking about stocks and things. I can't help them."

"Dad said you doubled his portfolio. And did it in less than two days. He said he wished he'd known you when he was younger...he might be as rich as Midas right now." She had. It had been easy. TJ had been willing to do whatever she said for him to do. "And I know that you work on Noah's investments as well. Did you know that Tanner is going on the same advice you told Dad? He said that once he gets enough money, he might open his own firm."

"Tanner needs a less aggressive and more long-term investment strategy. He has plenty of time to make money, while your dad wants to take your mom on a long.... What?" Trent just grinned at her. "That is not the same thing as being an investment banker. I'm merely helping out family."

"If you say so." If there was ever a time when she wanted to throat punch him, it was right now. "By the way, did you know that the pack is in need of a financial director? You should take it over. Make some long-term investments for the pack."

She told him she'd do it before she realized the trap. Being the director for the pack opened her up to all kinds of people coming to her for advice. As soon as the pack meeting was over, she was going to murder her new husband. Joe looked down at the rings on her hand.

Just over three hours ago they'd been wed. It hadn't been a big ceremony, just mostly family and a few of their friends, and it had been held in the field that served as the pack meeting place. The entire event had taken less than forty minutes, and she was now Mrs. Johanna Calhoun. She soon discovered that having five brothers was a little overwhelming in that they were more protective now than they had been before.

"Scott wants to know if you'll work with him." Scott was the only brother that had not kissed her after Trent claimed her. "He said to tell you that if you come and work in his office with him, he'll make it worth your while in donuts."

"I love donuts." It was a new thing for her. Usually one to avoid sweets as much as possible, she'd been turned on to pumpkin cookies and donuts in the same day, and she could not seem to get enough of both. "What does he do, anyway?"

She knew that Elijah was an investment guru, and had been having fun since he'd bought out Trent.

Sterling was still recovering from a horrific car accident that had killed two other people. He'd not been the one that caused it, but he had lost his job as a teacher when the pain had kept him from working. The college had needed someone to take the job now, and he'd not been able to do so. She knew that he still hurt from time to time, and Joe was pretty sure that he'd not told everyone everything that had happened. He looked like a man haunted by something horrific.

Tanner was currently unemployed, but looking. If he took the job that Noah was offering him, he'd be busier than he'd ever been, but he'd have the freedom that he'd not had as a lawyer in a firm. She, too, had hated being in an office all day, and was glad when she'd moved on to something more. Tanner was smart, personable, and he was a ladies' man. Joe wondered what the man would do when his own mate came along, and how the women he had in his harem would take it when he was off the market. It was going to be a great deal of fun watching the younger man get caught up in love.

Randal was a kindergarten teacher. She'd never seen a man more suited to the job than he was. He loved kids and was favored by them even after they left his classroom. Randal was also favored by the moms of the kids, and sometimes it got a little out of hand. She had to smile thinking about the other day, when he'd had to sic his mom on one particularly aggressive woman.

He'd been walking to his car, and his mom had been in hers just pulling in the lot to have dinner with her baby boy, she'd told her. Then this woman came out of her car and nearly tackled him to the ground. Randal had seen his mom coming toward them and had begged her to help him out. Christine had pulled the woman off her son and tore into the woman like she was five years old and caught stealing. Which, Joe supposed, she had been…stealing her baby boy.

Scott? She had no idea what he did, and looked at Trent when she realized he'd not answered her. "What is it? What are you not telling me?"

"Nothing bad. But Scott is an instructor." When he didn't elaborate, she asked him what sort of instructor. "He teaches couples how to have sex...you know, doms and subs, how to work their lifestyle out and become better partners. It's a process, I guess, and Scott is a natural at it."

"I don't understand. Doms and subs? You mean as in bondage and whips?" He told her that not all dom/sub relationships involved whips. "And this is what he does? And he wants me to come and work for him?"

"He said he'd like for you to come and be his receptionist. Scott assured me that you'd never be involved in the actual work he does." She tried to see if he was joking with her or not. "I know that you don't need the money, but it does pay well. And he said you can have stock options."

"You don't care that I'd be working in a...a sex shop?" Trent shrugged as he pulled her up from the chair and led her to the door. "I mean...really?"

"Yes, really. He wanted me to talk to you first, before you found out." She asked what his parents thought of it. "They don't care as long as he's happy and out of trouble."

She could see that too. The Calhouns loved their children without any sort of restrictions, and they supported them in whatever they needed to do to be happy. And they were, for the most part. She thought them to be very secure in what they did.

So, as they made their way out to their first pack meeting as husband and wife, and also pack leaders, she had to think of how to look Scott in the face and not wonder what sort of things he'd done that day. Giggling, she thought perhaps she'd ask him for a manual or something.

CHAPTER 11

Trent had been on this field several thousand times in his life. Each time had meant a great deal to him. But none were going to be as epic as this one would be. He was pack leader, and he had his mate at his side. As he entered the arena, he heard the hush move over the field and he had to smile. This was for him.

Trent wasn't a vain man. Nor was he one that wanted someone to pat him on the back, but he did love having not just Joe at his side, but his family there as well when he took this huge step. A change in his life that would last forever. When he stood upon the large stump that had been at one time the tree of life for their kind, he looked around. It was time.

"As you all know, Casey has been convicted of crimes that resulted in the death of several people. And even though he is dead, his name has been bandied about as a criminal. But that's not why I killed him. He was going to harm your alpha-bitch." The murmurs were loud but soon quieted again. "That day in the bank, I had no idea that he'd been a part of this. All I saw was him standing over my mate, his teeth bared and his hackles up. He meant to kill her."

Reaching out his hand, he brought Joe to the top with him. Holding her like this, as close as he could, all he could think about was how close he'd been to seeing her hurt. Not dead. Thankfully she could no more die than he could, but she could have been hurt badly all the same.

"Ladies and gentlemen, I'd like for you to meet my mate, Joe Calhoun. Your leader and master forever." The shout that started was deafening in the field. Flowers were tossed at them, some landing on them but mostly around them. They looked to be in a faerie garden. The ground was covered in the petals.

They were doing things differently this time. There would be a run, in which everyone who wanted to could shift and run freely in the fields. Not that there were any restrictions from that sort of thing normally, but tonight, with the moon full over them, it had a special magical quality to it. With a new pack master and his mate, there would not be the normal ritual of bringing forth issues and problems that had occurred during the time before, and no one would be brought to justice over some problems that were a result of it.

As he and Joe moved among the crowd, people stopped to talk to them, most offering congratulations and a few asking for a small token. It had been this way since he was a boy. The master and his mate would hand out favors, usually a small coin that could be returned when they had done a misdeed, and this would lessen their punishment. They each had ten, and after his were all gone, he looked to his dad, who was always close at hand.

"You did good." Trent smiled at his dad, never seeing him so happy before. "Right proud of you, I am. Your mom is too, but I'm about to bust with this."

"You always told me that I'd be here someday." He had, since his first changing. "I'm so glad that you were here with us when we took our first walk."

"My pleasure." He looked around like he didn't want someone to hear his next words. "That mate of yours, you know that there are some that are wondering if you'll change her too. I don't think she could get much more perfect, but they are asking."

"We talked about it, and we're waiting. I don't know what it will do to her, and there is little information on changing a day walker to a wolf. Noah said he'd ask around." His dad nodded and smiled. "You want to know something else? We're going to try to have a baby or two before the end of next year."

"Hot damn." They both looked around when the crowd hushed at his dad's loud voice. When he spoke again, he was much quieter, but no less excited. "That'll make your mom and me very happy. To have a grandbaby. I have to tell you, son, I despaired of you six ever getting around to it."

Hugging his dad, Trent felt his eyes fill with tears. He was as happy as he could be right now, and his dad was there for him too. It was weird, but over the last several days he'd been very emotional and had yet to ask Joe about it. He was sure it had something to do with the fact that they were so busy all the time. Seeing Noah walking toward him, he decided to ask him about it.

"It's overwhelming, isn't it?" Trent told him it was more than that. It was draining too. "It's because of the power you're getting. Not just from Joe but me as well. My blood, you see. When you took it, you took on more of me. Joe said she was having the same problems."

"Yes, she told me. I thought it was me feeling what she was." Noah said that was part of it but not all. "Will it level out, you think?"

"Oh yes. In about another decade or so."

Trent wasn't sure if he was kidding or not, but never got the chance to ask him. Two of his younger pack members came to him about an issue and he went with them to take care of it.

As soon as he entered the woods, he knew something was wrong. Running now, he kept up with the younger pups as they led him to Sterl. He could hear him then. His screams were tearing through him as if he was hurting too. Stopping the younger men, he asked them to go and get his mate and brothers.

"Don't tell my parents. Unless they ask. So don't go by them." Billy, the younger of the boys, nodded. "Get the others here now. And find Noah. He was in the field where you found me."

Going deeper into the woods alone now, he reached out to Sterl. He was in pain, he could feel it now, and it was a deep pain of his mind and heart that Trent didn't know how to fix. As soon as he saw his brother curled into a tight ball, Trent approached him slowly, speaking softly to him.

"Sterl, it's me, Trent. I'm here for you." The sob was heart wrenching, and he moved to touch him. "Tell me what I can do. Where do you hurt?"

"Everywhere." Trent could see that he'd cut his face and arms. While he didn't have any idea how that had happened, he knew that they were only superficial and nothing for him to worry about now. "Kill me. Please, end my life now."

"I can't do that." Tears blurred his vision as he touched the long scar that he knew was on his brother's back. "Come on, Sterl, let me pick you up and take you to the house."

"Don't touch me." He continued to run the scar, knowing that it pained him now because it was tight. "Trent, they made me an immortal. I can't live forever like this. Make them take it back. I don't want to live like this."

"I know. I'm so sorry. I know." He moved closer to Sterl and held him, like a mother would a child. He could hear his brothers coming and wasn't sure it was a good idea for anyone to see him like this. Then Noah appeared in front of him, and the noise from the woods his brothers were making stopped.

"I sent them back. I let them think it was a hoax. I didn't think you'd want it spread around that Sterl was in pain." Noah got down on his knees just as Joe came into the meadow where they were. "She and I are going to help you, Sterling."

"No. Just take the immortality from me and let me die." Noah didn't say anything as he tore open his vein. "That won't work. I've tried that before."

That shocked Trent. His brother had tried to get a vampire to take away his pain. He looked at Noah when he only shook his head and put his wrist to his mouth. As he did that, Joe pulled Sterl's wrist to her mouth and bit down. She was going to drain out whatever poison that Noah found. And he told Trent there was plenty.

About a year ago now, Sterl and four of his friends had been out on a date. He'd been the odd man out, but had gone anyway when his date, a human, had gotten ill and wasn't able to go with him. Sterl never drank alcohol but told him later that there had been something in the tea he'd been drinking. Something that had made him dizzy and sick with it.

"I was just sipping it when I felt the urge to throw up. I thought it was the food we'd eaten. No one else was sick or dizzy, so I went outside to get some fresh air to see if that helped." Sterl had been in his own bed then, having been released from the hospital that morning. He'd asked to speak to him alone and told him what had happened. "Then when we all got into the car to leave, Mitch said he was feeling great and had promised us all that he'd not drank either. I believed him because I didn't smell it on him."

"What happened then?" Sterl hadn't looked like he was going to answer, so Trent started to change the subject. Sterl's face was cut up, his back the worst of it, having been thrown from the car, despite his seat belt, and impaled on a tree. Plus, his leg had been broken in several places. No one then or now could figure out why the wounds didn't go away when he'd shifted, nor had the bruising lessened. It was as if he were a human and not a wolf.

"A woman—or something—was in front of the car. Like she just appeared. I don't mean like she ran in front of us, but she was just there. Mitch swerved hard to the right, which should have put us in the ditch rather than.... I felt the car lift up, and then it was falling over the hillside like we were in a ball being rolled head over ass." Sterl looked away as he finished. "I woke up, hanging from the tree with my feet in front of me, and I could see that I was broken. Not hurt...I was literally broken from the accident. And there it was again. Like a woman, but not. I thought that I'd only dreamt about it being there when we'd wrecked...the woman, I mean. But there she was again."

"What was she doing?" Sterl again said nothing for several minutes, and that time Trent had waited. He thought that the pain of the injuries had made Sterling see the woman, but after he continued, he knew he'd seen the thing.

"Mitch was hanging out of the front window. His body was moving, I could see it. When this thing stood in front of him, he reached for her, begging her to help him. She reached out her hand and touched him. But instead of helping him, she jerked him from the broken window and tore him in half. Just tore him apart. She moved to Bri then. Her body was on the ground behind the car. The thing, this woman thing, killed her too. Tore her head off and left it to lay there." Sterl looked at him then. The anguish of what he'd seen was there on his face. "Tony and Beth were next. The thing stabbed a large piece of the glass from the broken windows into his chest, going not just into him but completely through him. Beth was dead. I could see that her neck was snapped, but the thing didn't stop. She walked to her and did the same thing, using a large stone to crush her head."

"Christ." Trent hadn't wanted to ask him about what she'd done to him. He hoped that she'd left him there, thinking that he was going to die anyway. But Sterl had started crying then, sobbing out the rest of his tale.

"She came to me then. Just levitated up the tree to me." Trent held his breath. "As she floated in front of me, I got a good look at her face. She was...she was beautiful. Long dark hair, lips that were full and red. Her body, sheathed in this sort of transparent aura, was gorgeous. She just stared at me until...until...."

He'd looked away then, as if he were too frightened to continue. Trent wasn't sure he wanted to know what she'd done. Was positive even to this day that the thing that had killed his friends had meant the same for Sterl.

"Her fingers seemed to morph, like ours do when we shift. But they elongated, and her nails darkened until I was sure they were covered in old blood and were as long as her arm. Her hair, too, changed. It lightened to a purest white and hung below her feet. Her face seemed to shrink in on itself, until she was nothing more than bones with something stretched tautly over her skull. When she touched me, stuck her nails through me, I could see that she was enjoying it, and I had the sudden urge to just die, to give up. But then she spoke." Sterl looked away again. "She told me that I was going to be her biggest prize as yet. That my seed would flood the earth with demons."

Sterl lay back, his eyes closed as Trent held his hand. He hadn't even realized that he'd touched him until he felt his brother's fingers tighten around his. They sat there, neither of them speaking, as the sun lowered in the sky and the sounds of the outdoors echoed in the house.

"I'm never going to meet my mate, Trent. I never want to have children. I don't want that thing to come back and take them from me." Trent asked him if that was what she'd said to him. "Yes. My children are going to be hers."

~~~

Memories not his own hit his mind. Noah knew who the she-devil was and what she'd done to the man in front of him. Sterling Calhoun was lucky to be alive. As he filtered through the terror of the young wolf and focused on the words she'd said to him, Noah also felt the man's resolve not to ever find or keep his mate. He'd rather die lonely than to take the chance that any issue of the union would be taken from him. Noah looked at Joe.

I know her. He nodded and asked her not to speak of it here. *Can you help him? Can we keep him safe?*

We will.

As Sterling drank his blood, Noah moved into his mind and pushed the poison from his body. He knew as surely as he was helping this man that the she-devil had put a poison in not just his mind, but his body as well. Noah found all that he could, knowing that if he didn't get it all, the man would try to talk him into letting him die again. And knowing what he did now, Noah wasn't sure that he'd not help him.

When Sterling had drank all that Noah could give him, Noah pulled his wrist away and sealed the wound. He'd have to go and feed now. Helping Sterling had drained him more than he wanted to admit. But he'd be healthier, if not a little happier, now that the poison was gone from him. Noah turned to Trent after putting Sterling into a deep sleep of the dead.

"He will need to be watched over. I've put him deep, far deeper than he's ever been before." Trent nodded and told him he'd do it. "He won't wake for a week. Then at the end of that time, he will need to shift to rid himself of the scars that have been a part of him for far too long. And then I would suggest that he rest. He will need it, but will be most...make sure that he rests."

"I will." Noah knew that Trent would too. The man was Sterling's pack master now, and would resort to commanding that he rest if Sterling didn't comply. Noah looked at Joe when she said nothing. "This other vampire, the one he tried to get to help him, do you know who it was?"

He did. "He is dead. He was murdered some weeks ago."

Noah would bet anything that not only had the man been murdered by the same she-devil that had hurt Sterling, but that she'd killed him because he'd tried to help him. Noah wasn't worried. He was much more powerful than her, and he knew something that she didn't. Noah was aware of her now.

As he took to the skies to find someone to feed from, Noah thought about the woman. She'd done this before. Attacked without provocation. Killed without thought, and had tried her best to repopulate the world with someone like Sterling. The prime of a pack, the strongest of a wolf family. But she'd gotten the wrong one this time; not only had she not picked the alpha, but she'd picked Noah's family. Noah was very protective of what he considered his.

Will she come here now? Noah had to smile at Joe's question. *She'll be aware that someone helped him. Do you suppose she'll come here and try to reclaim him?*

Yes. He moved above the trees and then landed on a particularly high branch to watch the humans below him. There were several, and he'd need at least three of them to fill up. Noah didn't kill, but he would need a great deal from these men before he was healthy again. *It is her bad fortune that she has tried to take Sterling. It will land her in the middle of my realm, and that will get her killed once and for all.*

She's dangerous. More than that, she's power hungry and strong. How will you defeat her, Noah? You have tried before. He had. And he knew that he'd not given it his best. It had been a half-assed effort at best. *If she comes here, and I'm betting she will, what will she do to Sterling now that he's no longer her pawn?*

We are stronger than we were. And as a family, you know as well as I do that we gain from that too. Sterling has you and me now. He will be all right. She does not know that with my blood, she cannot harm him again. And with your powers surrounding him, she won't find him an easy target as she did before. He thought about the images in Sterling's mind. *She went there for him. Gave him an elixir that was to put him into a deep sleep while she killed the others. It is going to come back to harm her that he not only knows what she did, but that he remembers her despite her trying to take the memories from him.*

We know her now as well. Noah moved to the ground, watching for someone to come up behind him as he commanded the men to stand still. Drinking from them, just enough to sustain himself for another time, he was forever careful that no one snuck up on him. When he was finished, he took some cash from his pocket and lined those of the men he'd used. It would do him no good anyway, and he wanted to repay them for their help. *I will put out a call to arms for others. We'll all keep an eye out for her, and make sure that wherever she's hiding, it will be reported to us soon.*

After closing the connection to Joe, he moved to his home. Michael was there, waiting for him as he'd asked him to do. When he handed Noah the file he'd asked for, Michael sat down and began snapping green beans, a thing that he'd never seen him do before.

"Mr. Marshall is staying here. And I thought it would be fun to make food for him. I was not aware that it was so much work." Noah started to point out that most of the things he'd eaten long ago were now available in cans, but thought he'd just let him figure it out. It might be fun for a while to watch him struggle with it. "Also, we have a new phone. One that hangs on the wall. And Internet capabilities. Mr. Marshall asked for it, and I saw no problem with having it put into the household. Is that all right?"

"It is. You do whatever he needs to make him feel like this is his home." Michael nodded, and Noah was almost afraid to bring up the she-devil. "Sterling Calhoun has been touched by Helenia."

Noah was just able to grab the bowl filled with the newly snapped beans before it hit the floor. Michael stood up but sat down again twice before he asked him where she was. He assured him that he had no idea at the moment.

"Does he know what she is? What she's done?" Noah told him what he'd seen in the younger man's memories. "Oh, that poor boy. That poor, poor boy. We'll have to protect him, my lord. Keep him safe, and his family."

"I'm doing that now. I've put out a call to the Board of Vampires, and they're to let me know when they have information I can use. I'm afraid, as is Joe, that she has harmed him thinking that she's gotten the alpha. When she figures it out, no one will be safe." Michael said he agreed as well. "I've healed him, giving him a great part of me so that he'll be protected. Joe will do the same for Trent. Here, we'll have to remain on our toes to make sure that she doesn't get by us."

"I assure you, sir, she will not be able to get by us. I will make sure that all of the house is safe from her. I will call in a few favors today to make sure." Noah smiled. He didn't even want to know who might owe him favors. As he said his good days, he made his way to his lair. Things were going quickly now, and he needed to be rested.

Before You Go...

HELP AN AUTHOR

write a review

THANK YOU!

Share your voice and help guide other readers to these wonderful books. Even if it's only a line or two your reviews help readers discover the author's books so they can continue creating stories that you'll love. Login to your favorite retailer and leave a review. Thank you.

AWARD WINNING, BESTSELLING AUTHOR

Kathi Barton, author of the bestselling series Force of Nature, lives in Nashport, Ohio with her husband Paul. In addition to writing full time Kathi likes to spend time with her eight grandkids, three children and three children-in-laws. She writes to relax and have fun.

Her muse, a cross between Jimmy Stewart and Hugh Jackman brings them to life for her readers in a way that has them coming back time and again for more. Her favorite genre is paranormal romance with a great deal of spice. You can visit Kathi on line and drop her an email if you'd like. She loves hearing from her fans. aaronskiss@gmail.com.

Follow Kathi on her blog:
http://kathisbartonauthor.blogspot.com/

www.ingramcontent.com/pod-product-compliance
Lightning Source LLC
Chambersburg PA
CBHW032137170626
46808CB00006B/2268